Self-Storage Wars

A Peek Behind The Front-lines

By

Ginger Monastyrski

Dedication

This book is dedicated to John T Mutchner. He has been the greatest boss a person could ever ask for. It was with his encouragement that I recorded all these stories and turned them into a book. Here's to 18 more years!

Table of Contents

Preface

I have worked in the self-storage industry for more than eighteen years. One would think that a parking lot full of garages wouldn't create much drama. I realized, where there are people, there will always be drama.

Each of these stories are recounted to the best of my ability. As insane as many of them may sound, these are each an account of the craziness that I have encountered over the years of being a captive audience in my office. Everything from unwanted sexual advances to downright criminal behavior is included in the collection of short stories.

I often tell someone what happens during a typical day and their response is, "No way!" Considering these responses, I thought that you might want to hear a few of my tales as well.

So sit back and enjoy.

Chapter 1 Crazies

Kidnapped

Early on, I realized that this job wouldn't be dull. I assumed that taking care of a bunch of garages full of household items in a huge parking lot couldn't be that hard. I was so wrong.

One beautiful spring day, I was sitting in my office with my friend Jim when I got a phone call. I answer, and a man says, whispering into the phone, "Listen. I've watched enough CSI to know what I'm talking about, so listen. A woman is being held against her will in unit 120. I hear her screaming for help and banging on the door to be let out." I managed only one facility at the time, so I quickly narrowed it down to this location. My friend, Jim, was in the office with me. I told him that I was going outside for a minute and would be right back. I walked out and continued talking on the phone; I proceeded down the aisle toward unit 120. I started asking the guy on the telephone if he lives nearby and if that's why he can hear her. In the meantime, I looked around to ensure no one was purposely luring me outside. I notice one of the nearby neighbors peeking around a curtain at a sliding patio door while talking on his phone.

Bingo! There's my guy. I ask him, "Is that you in the door there?" He quickly ducks back behind the curtain. I said, "That's okay. I saw you. No reason to hide." I continue, "I am standing outside unit 120 and don't hear anyone." I even knocked on the door to appease him and asked if anyone was there. He screams, "Don't lie to me. I've been lied to before and know what I'm talking about. I heard a woman in there, but she's quiet now. Maybe she's drugged." I explained to him that I would keep an eye on the unit. I told him I'd watch for anyone coming or going from the place and ensure nothing odd was happening.

Suddenly, he screams into the phone, "Watch out behind you!" I turned around, and my friend Jim was standing behind me. He had walked out of the office to check on me. I said, "It's okay. He's a friend of mine." I was trying so hard not to laugh. It was like a scene from a horror movie. He finally let me off the phone after assuring him I would follow up on unit 120.

It turns out, sadly, that he had recently changed medications and was having horrible side effects. I found this out by asking another neighbor about him. The female neighbor told me he had sexually propositioned her husband several days earlier. This was not normal for him, and they eventually found out what was causing his erratic behavior. It's been fifteen years, and I've never had the opportunity to speak with this neighbor again. I assume they got his meds straightened out, and all is well with him.

Tin Foil Hat Lady

I got two stories in one with this next customer. I knew something was a little off when she first rented from me. A few days later, she confirmed my suspicions. She came into the office and told me someone had snooped around in her storage unit. I asked her if the lock was missing, and she said, "No." I asked if anyone else had a key to the storage unit, and again, she replied, "No."

I asked her if anyone knew her gate code. Again, she replied, "No." I asked her how she could tell someone was messing around with her storage unit. She said, "I think someone is trying to play with my head. They are trying to drive me crazy. Someone is going into my storage unit and moving things around. Just enough to make me think I'm losing my mind."

I suggested she put a second lock on her unit alongside the original one, just to be sure, and change the gate code. If someone had her unit number and gate code, we could stop them by changing her information. She agreed and proceeded to write her new gate code on the back of one of my business cards sitting on the desk. Her handwriting was atrocious. I took the card and read the number back to her to ensure I was reading it correctly.

All of a sudden, she loses it. She yelled, "Oh my god! You read it out loud!" I told her it was okay. We were the only two people in the office. She grabbed her cell phone and held it to her chest and whispered, "Don't you know they bug our phones?" That's when the lightbulb came on and I realized we were having a tinfoil hat moment. I asked her to write another code on the card and promised not to say it aloud this time. You know, encase our phones were bugged.

I hadn't heard anything from her for a week or two. She rented in my climate-controlled building in the first unit next to the door. One day, I just happened to be sweeping and checking the units while she was tinkering around in her storage. I opened the door to the climate-controlled building, and her door was open about halfway. This behavior is normal for my more paranoid customers. They always believe people are casing their units, trying to see what's in there. They close the doors, with just a foot or so open at the bottoms, to keep people from seeing their stuff. So the almost closed door didn't set off any alarm bells under the circumstances; however, the sound of someone crawling overhead in the duct-work did. I could hear she was just a few feet away from her unit but up in the ceiling. I called out her name and asked her what she was doing up there. She asked me to hold on a minute and would come down to talk to me.

She made her way out of the ceiling and crawled between the metal railings where the duct-work for the heating and cooling comes into each unit directly above the roll-up doors inside each storage room. She said, "I had to climb up there to show that someone could get into my unit through the ceiling and mess with my stuff." This woman was extremely thin. She was underweight but tall and skinny. I am afraid that she had the look of a meth addict. I didn't feel like she was doing meth at the time she was renting with me but was suffering the consequences of doing so, being very flighty, antsy, jumpy, and paranoid. I asked her not to climb up there again; as far as I know, she never tried. Luckily, the paranoia got the best of her, and she moved out less than two months later. She was a prime example of where I felt like I had to keep an eye on the customer while they were at the facility for the customers' health and safety.

Schizo Lady

Recently, I dealt with a woman who had schizophrenia. That day, in particular, was not going very well. I don't remember most of what went on that day that made it such a bad day, but I know I had to deal with several rude and pushy customers, and I had issues with two of my facilities having technical problems. When it rains, it pours, and that day was a hurricane of bad.

I answered the phone to a woman who, right out of the gate, is copping a major attitude. Using the word "Listen..." as in, "Listen. This is what you are going to do for me." I often wonder if people think that talking to someone like that will help their case. It makes me want to shut down and be less sympathetic to their plight. She came at me with both barrels loaded and wanted to pick a fight. She had gotten a late notice, and it had pissed her off. She didn't 'appreciate getting a letter like that. I explained that I sent those out to folks so they understood that I didn't get their payment. It might have gotten lost in the mail or was just an oversight. It was much better to get a letter in the mail when you are only one month behind than to wait two or three months and have a much bigger problem.

My explanation just managed to piss her off even more. She was now threatening to move out and give me a bad review. I was unsure how it would read. *Don't ever rent here because they send you a reminder notice when you don't pay your bill!*

She continued to get angrier and angrier and soon was cussing me out. She wasn't claiming that she had sent the payment. She was mad that I would ask her to pay when she hadn't. After being cussed a few more times and seeing that I wasn't getting anywhere and the threats began to escalate, I hung up.

Perhaps, five minutes later, the phone rang again; She was calling back. This time, she took on the most sticky-sweet sarcastic tone she could muster. "Oh, sorry about that; let's try it this way and see if it helps." Again, speaking in a very sappy over-the-top condescending way. "I'll tell you what, let me give you my credit card number, and you take care of my bill. Do you think you can do that?"

I said, "Sure. Go ahead with your card number." She began reading her card number, one number at a time, with a long pause in between. She was doing this to show me that she thought I was a moron and that she needed to read the numbers very slowly and loudly for me to comprehend them. Finally, she got the whole number out, and with prompting, she gave me the expiration date and CVV code from the back of her card. The entire time, she was reading it in the sappiest syrupy sweet, and snarky voice. Right as I was ending the phone call, she muttered something under her breath, but at that point, I didn't bother to ask her what she had said. I was done with the phone call and eager to get her off the line.

A few days later, she called again. Having worked in this business and the business of customer service for many years, I have become rather good at telling when I'm being put on. However, in this case, I honestly believed that this woman had no memory of having called me three days prior. She asked me if she owed that month's rent and, if not, when her rent was due again. I told her that she was paid up-to-date due to the payment she had made just three days before. She had no recollection of calling me. She was just as nice and friendly as a customer would typically be, just calling in to confirm a payment had been made. I told her the phone call from three days ago paid for this month's rent and the missed payment from the last month. She said, "Oh, good. I couldn't remember if I paid this month and figured I'd better call you and make sure." She couldn't remember she had called me twice that day. The first call was where she screamed, cussed, and threatened me, and the second was where she faked a sticky-sweet voice and finally made the payment. I think she was either off her medications or suffered from a mental disorder and seriously had no idea she had called. The thing is, she had made my day just awful. Starting your day with someone screaming at you and cussing you out is bad enough but in the end, she didn't even remember making those calls.

Go figure.

Fight Between Two Hoarders

Nothing says good morning like a couple of customers about to duke it out when you pull into the parking lot. What an excellent way to start the day. As I drove into the parking lot of my office, I saw two customers standing in the middle of the drive having an animated conversation. I could tell right away they were arguing . Before I could even get parked and out of my car, they ran up to my window, and one yelled, "Thank god you're here. You can settle this."

These two lovelies were just about ready to start throwing punches. The irony was that one was an older black woman and the other a heavy male home care professional. The last two people on the face of the Earth that I would have figured would be in a fight in my driveway. They had a couple of things in common. Both had multiple units, were slightly off-kilter, and both were hoarders.

They should have been comparing notes on their junk collections but, instead, were about to rip each other's heads off. When I got out of my car, I went straight to my office door to put my things away with both in tow. Each was yelling their side of the story. Customer #1 had pulled up in front of the door and entry keypad to look at my office hours displayed on the door, slightly blocking the way for customer #2 to be able to key in her number without having to walk more than ten steps. That point was the catalyst, being vitally essential, and would soon cause a huge fight. She exited her car and began screaming at Customer #1.

Customer #2 said, "Why do you have to park your fat lazy ass right in front of the damn keypad? I shouldn't have to walk around your car to enter my code."

Customer #1 answered, "I was only looking to see the office hours. You are the one being a lazy ass. Why can't you just walk up to the keypad?"

Customer #2 asked , "What did you just call me?"

Customer #1 answered, "Nothing, you didn't call me first!"

Customer #2 said, "Well, pencil dick, how about you get the fuck out of the way, you lazy ass cracker."

Customer #1 answered, "Why are you calling me a cracker? I didn't make a racist comment to you."

Customer #2 said, "Well, the only reason I can think of you sitting here blocking my way is 'cause you're a racist mother fucker."

Customer #1 answered, "Lady, I am the least racist person you will ever meet. I was once married to a black woman."

Customer #2 said, "Well, obviously, you couldn't please her with your little dick because you ain't married to her no more."

Customer #1 answered, "I have half a mind to show you that I am not little, but I won't."

I had arrived just in time to keep customer #1 from exposing himself to customer #2 to show her that his privates were indeed not little, thus debunking the myth of why he and his wife had split. How did it come to this, from someone parking in front of the keypad to racist accusations and DE-emasculating comments? Amazingly, they both managed to scream the same story to me. They admitted to saying what the other accused them of, and I just shook my head. I can only imagine what might have happened if these two had gone at each other in the Covid-19/2016 Political climate.

Crime tape may have been needed.

Chapter 2 Liars

All Nine Lives and Then Some

My customers rarely come up with inventive excuses for why they are again paying the bill late. Sometimes they use the same excuse over and over again. At the least, they should keep a little lie Journal so they don't use the same lie excessively. If you can't be inventive and come up with new ones, at least stagger them and try not to use the same excuse two months in a row. Be more creative for once.

One of the excuses that I have been given include the following.

My cat died. This young woman's cat had died multiple times. Each time she would call and act extremely distraught. She would already be crying before she even called and whenever I would answer the phone, she would work up her tears and sob to be at peak efficiency. She would go into a long story about how her cat became ill and she had to take him to the vet. The vet bill would always be in the hundreds of dollars, causing her not to have enough money to pay the rent. She would promise to pay later in the month and express how she hoped she wouldn't have a late fee since her cat died. I would make a few notations on her account. "Cat died, big vet bill, will be paid late." Just a simple note to show she had at least contacted us. She would almost always call back later in the month and make the payment. Occasionally, it would carry over to the next month.

Each time she called to tell me her payment would be late, it was because her cat had gotten sick and died. . Month after month, she would tell me about some new ailment her cat had contracted. She mentioned the cat by name, ruling out she had numerous cats that all seemed to have met an untimely death. Each time, she would go into detail about the cat's illness and how it was very costly, and she would pay later in the month or as soon as she had the money. Again, I would make a note on her account. It reached the point where I was typing, "Her cat died again."

This lady's cat did indeed have nine lives and used them all.

Grandma Dies for the 6th Time.

Then there was the young lady whose Grandmother died. She called to tell me that her Grandma had passed away and she had to go out of town for the funeral. She said that travel expenses would cause her to be late with the rent. On top of that, she had to pay for the funeral. She was a very young girl, perhaps 19 or so. I thought it was quite a lot to expect a child to pay for the Grandmother's funeral, but maybe they were close, and there were no other relatives. A couple of months go by. She has paid for that month's rent and the one after that. However, she called at the beginning of the third month to let me know that her Grandmother had died. She will have to travel out of town for the funeral, and she is the only one that can pay for the funeral expenses. Okay. That's a little odd. Both of her grandmothers had died, leaving her behind to pay for their funerals.

Unlikely but not wholly impossible. She called and paid the bill late, and again a month or two went by before she called to let me know that she would be paying her bill late because, yep, you guessed it, her Grandma died. She is the only relative in a position to pay for the funeral, but it will make things tight for a month or two. However, she will catch up on the bill as soon as possible. This is her third dead Grandma. All of which she has had to take on the burden of burying. This happened once more before she finally packed up her things and moved out.

I wondered if this was her only excuse for every life situation. "I'm sorry, Babe, I'm not in the mood; Grandma died."

I Smell An Insurance Scam

I have some customers that like to claim that they have been robbed to get a payout from their insurance. I guess if they want to commit fraud, that's on them. It only makes all of our insurance rates go up when many people think of making false claims, and in addition to that, my facility gets a bad rep. When the police report is made, people associate the facility with the information they heard or read. For these reasons alone, I'd like people to stop acting like scumbags.

One of these lovely folks came in one afternoon and drove to his storage unit. He was back there for about 3 minutes before he came up to the office. He told me that he had been robbed. I was out in the facility earlier checking doors and looking for move-outs. No locks were missing, and no signs of any break-ins. He insisted that I walk out to the unit with him. I asked him if he had locked his door correctly, and he said he had.

He said, "I guess they picked the lock and put it back on again." With the round disc locks, they would have had to pick it again to put it back on. In my nearly 18 years in the business, I've never had such a considerate thief as to secure the door again when they leave with your stuff. But I guess this was a first. He pulled up the door, pointed to a spot in the unit, and told me that he had a Zero Turn Radius Kubota mower in there, and somebody had taken it. The only place on the floor was the same size as a milk crate. A space so small that only a 12 x 12 square would have fit in it. The rest of the storage unit was packed with stuff wall to wall. He told me he would call the police and file an insurance claim. That was the first time someone had announced they were filing an insurance claim. Not unheard of but rare enough that it struck me as odd. He had coincidentally given me his ten-day notice two days before the robbery. So he was about to leave the storage unit when suddenly the world's smallest

Kubota mower came up missing from his storage unit. The police officer stopped by my office to ask a few questions about the guy. I could tell that he thought the guy was a fraud. I led him a little by saying, "He asked me to come out and look at his storage unit with him just before you arrived and showed me where the mower had been." The officer said, "I'm not convinced it was ever there. No grass, no tire marks anywhere, and there wasn't any room for one." I agreed with him, and we laughed at the fact that this guy pointed to this 12 x 12 spot and explained that the mower had sat there. I assume that at some point, he had owned the mower and probably had a receipt for it or pictures, but had sold it. This way, he gets two paydays for the price of one out of the mower.

Chapter 3 Unwanted Advances and Sexual Oddballs

I now have a Glock with me at all times. I should have had it with me a long time ago when I was younger, when more of this happened to me. I only recently got one because the world seems to have gotten a bit more dangerous the past few years. I just feel more secure having it with me because I'm alone in the office most of the time. There has rarely been a time when a guy has come into my office and just flirted with me and struck up a conversation. You know, the usual way people are supposed to interact - how a guy should act if he is interested and wants to see if it's mutual. Not with me. It goes from a smile to complete freaky situations in seconds. I believe that this is due mostly to me being alone in the office and no one is around to witness their behavior. The following stories are whatever in the heck qualifies as apparent flirting when men are around me in the office

What a "Jerk"

This handsome and well-spoken business owner would come into my office and chat with me from time to time while making his monthly payments. Weeks go by, the flirting continues, and I decide it's time to nip this in the bud. The next time he comes in, I didn't even get out of my desk chair to chat with him, hoping to send the message that he only needs to come into the office if he is doing business.

One day he came in and went straight to the restroom just to the side of the office. He calls for me to come to take a look at something. He sounds as if there is a giant spider or water leak, and I need to look at it immediately. I walked around the end of the counter to see him jerking off into the bathroom sink. His pants are around his hips, and he is wanking off into the sink. *What the hell*! was the only thing that came to mind. This was his 'next move?' He had gone through the preliminary flirty chatting at the desk stage and moved right into the jerk-off into her sink phase. Who in their right mind thinks, "I know how to impress? I'll jerk off here in the bathroom with the door open and call her over. She won't be able to resist my charm. "

I think these stunts never seem to phase me because I have become so jaded and desensitized by them. I seriously shrug them off as another day in the mental ward that is my world. After walking over to see what he wanted me to see, I said, "Don't make a mess in there." I had spoken in a tone that someone might use to speak to a 15-year-old boy they accidentally walked in on masturbating. I strolled over and opened the exit door to show him that he should leave now, and he did. Not another word was spoken about it, and he rarely says more to me than a simple greeting as he goes through the gate.

There is an update to this tale. It's been eight years since this story took place. As I mentioned, he says "Hello" in passing and rarely comes (No pun intended) into my office. Recently, he came to the office and wanted to show me his new vehicle. I had gotten a new car a few months back, and now my customer showed me that he had purchased the exact vehicle. He told me he would be getting a few things done, including a couple of add-ons. After that, his car would look exactly like mine. We're not talking about a cheap car here, either. This was a $50,000 stalker-y move. Now that was creepy.

To Kiss Or Not To Kiss

One of my most persistent customers was also one of the biggest jerks I've ever met. This guy wasn't attractive. He spoke in a very annoying, fast, and scattered manner. He had far more confidence than could ever be accredited to his looks. But for all his shortcomings, he was persistent.

The day after renting a storage unit from me, he returned to the office to buy a lock. I had to go into the back room to grab another box of locks as I had run out under the counter. I entered the back room, grabbed a box of locks, and turned around to see him standing inches from me. His breath was so bad and it was all I could smell.

In what he thought was a sultry voice, he asked, "Do you know how hard it is not to kiss you right now?"

I replied, "Do you know how hard I would knee you in the balls if you tried?"

He stepped back a step or two and then nervously laughed like it was all a big joke and he was just playing around. I returned with the box of locks and sold him one. He never entirely went to that level again but never gave up. He consistently flirted with me. I never once said or did anything to give him any indication that it was mutual. I began saying some pretty snarky things back to him. He never got the hint. Over the ten years, he rented with me, he would have his unit up for auction and pay it off at the last minute. Every three months, like clockwork, he was up for auction again. He would insist on coming into the office to ask for the balance on his account rather than simply calling.

For a short time, he dated a girl that had cancer. He did nothing but complain about her. He said, "She wasn't putting out like she used to." He had moved all her things into his storage unit and had her paying the bill for a while. His account was paid on time until she got too sick to work. He came into the office to tell me that he had 'dumped' her, and her dad was coming to get her stuff out of storage. Lovely guy.

The next girlfriend also paid the bill for a while. He would bring her into the office and then openly flirt with me. He was trying to piss her off. I don't know if he thought she might try to fight with me over this slug of a human being. She never took the bait and acted like this was standard operating procedure, and she would sit on the couch in my office and play with her phone. Maybe he was trying to get her attention away from the phone. It wasn't working. I knew they had broken up when his bill started going delinquent again.

I was never so happy when he finally went to auction. I had seen what was in his storage unit many times and even offered to give him some trash bags to throw the stuff into, and I would get rid of it for him when the dump truck came. All he had in there for all those years were some dirty clothing strung out all over the floor and some paperwork. It was never worth keeping. He would pay off the large balance with all the late fees each time, knowing that nothing in that unit was worth saving. He used the unit as an excuse to come to the office and bug the hell out of me.

Finally, after years of putting up with him, the unit was sold at auction. He had received the late notices and signed the auction notice. He was well aware that the unit had been sold at auction. However, that didn't stop him from showing up at the gate two months later, asking if he could come in and talk about his storage unit. I left him outside the gate and told him that the unit was gone now and there was nothing to discuss.

That was a great day.

He just called two weeks ago and asked the current price for a

10 x 10. I recognized his voice and told him that we wouldn't be able to rent to him again because he had gone to auction. He said, "That was a long time ago!" I thought, "Not long enough."

Heart Attack Guy

Perhaps one of the oddest encounters I have ever had occurred right after being a good Samaritan. I used another post office years ago. I changed post offices later due to convenience. However, the original location was just a tiny post office. The outer lobby was 7 feet by 10 feet. This lobby area was where all the post office boxes were located. To the left of the mailboxes was a walk-in lobby through another set of glass doors. The postal person on duty that day has now retired, but she was one of my favorites. She was so efficient and knowledgeable. She knew everyone by name and box number.

Just as the weather was beginning to get chilly outside, I went into the post office to get the storage facility's mail from the box. A little man was standing next to me. He stood 5 ft 2 or so. He was a wiry guy, around 40 years old. He, too, was getting his mail, and I had seen him a few times before. His schedule must have been about the same as mine, and we picked our mail up for our respective businesses at about the same time each morning. I walked into the lobby this day and saw him getting his mail. I might have said, "Good Morning." or mentioned the weather turning cooler.

I noticed that he had a strained look on his face. He looked as if he were in pain. Pretty soon, he put one of his hands up against the mailboxes to steady himself. I asked if he was okay, and he said, "I think I might be having a heart attack." He started taking off his jacket. I quickly asked him to sit down, and he did. He immediately wanted to lay down, so I helped him to the floor and placed his jacket under his head. Trying to make him comfortable, I got down on my knees next to him and held his hand. He was scared and in a fit of panic. That is normal behavior from someone who thinks they might be having a heart attack. I had left my phone in the car, so I stood up, knocked on the back room door, and asked the postal lady to call an ambulance for him. I went back and sat with him and tried to assure him that he would be okay and keep him as calm as possible. I didn't want him to exasperate the problem.

Soon enough, the ambulance showed up and took over. He never lost consciousness while I was there and only needed someone to stay with him until the ambulance arrived. I left and made a mental note to ask the postal lady later if she had an update on him. It would be a simple wellness check to see if he was okay.

About a week later, I arrived at the post office a little later than expected, and the lobby was open. I asked the postal woman if she knew anything about his condition. Of course, she knew all about him. She knew his name and where he worked, and he had contacted her to tell her that someone else would be picking up the mail for a while. He had had a heart attack and was taking some time off work. She mentioned that he was happy that someone had been with him and was glad he wasn't alone. I figured that was the end of that, and I would most likely see him in the post office again sometime when he was doing better, that is if he was allowed to return to work.

Weeks go by, and out of the blue, this little guy is outside my gate at the North office, ringing the buzzer on the keypad. My office is behind the gate at this location. I recognize him and activate the gate so he can come to the office. He walked into the office and very awkwardly thanked me for helping him. He said he had never had the slightest chest pain before that day, which made this an even more terrifying experience for him. I told him that I was glad I could help. He said, "I just wanted to come by and say thanks. If it's okay with you, can I give you a hug?"

"Well, of course," I said. I saw this as a show of gratitude. The man wanted to show me that he was thankful for my kindness.

Wrong! That may be how it started. It happened in literally less than a minute. I walked around my desk, hugged him, and said, "I'm glad it turned out okay and you are feeling better now." I was abruptly cut off in mid-sentence. He had gone in for the hug and immediately started humping my leg. Like a chihuahua on cocaine! I was shocked. I was so caught off guard that for perhaps three seconds or so, I just stood there. Then, just as fast as it started, it was over. He pulled away from me with a huge stain on the front of his work uniform. He looked at me like he was just as surprised and rushed out the front door. I quickly walked over to the gate controller and opened the gate to let him out of the facility.

I just stood there momentarily, shocked, and then started laughing. I thought, *Is this what you get for helping someone?* I stood there for a few minutes, then sat at my desk. I started thinking about calling someone to tell them what had happened. I didn't call the police. I don't know why. I don't know if it was the absurdness of what had happened or if somehow I knew that this little guy had mental issues. I realize now that I should have called the police, but at the time, the situation was so absurd that I didn't even want to talk to anyone about it.

A while later, I did go to the post office and talked to the postal lady. She said he had come in and asked if she knew who I was and how he could contact me to thank me. I told her exactly how he had 'thanked me,' and she was flabbergasted. She was apologizing all over the place, and now I was standing in the post office trying to console the upset clerk and letting her know it was okay, I was fine, and that she couldn't have had any idea that that would happen. I asked her not to give any information about me or where to find me to anyone else in the future.

No good deed goes unpunished.

$2500 For Sex

You meet all kinds of people in this job, some great people and some strange ones. This next story is one about a REALLY strange one.

Customer K came to my office about three years ago. He seemed to be a perfectly normal, friendly, and respectable guy. He was a local business owner and looking for storage for his business. He was a nice-looking guy and looked like he worked out. It came as a complete shock to me when he began flirting. I mean over-the-top, straightforward flirting. I'm at least ten years older than him, if not more. I told him right up front that I was married and not interested. He took this as a personal challenge on his part.

Every woman is flattered when a man flirts with them and finds them attractive, but this escalated quickly. He started asking me to sit next to him on the couch I have in my office, and I declined the offer. I probably said I was busy and needed to get back to work. He sat on the couch and patted the seat next to him, and I kept declining. Pretty soon, I said, "You need to go now." He left and called shortly after, asking if I was madathim.

He didn't return to the office or call for a long time. Months went by before he came back around again. Once again, he tried to get me to sit on the couch with him, and I refused. I barely escaped him, trying to grab my butt while I walked past him, and I once again asked him to leave. I came right out and asked him what his problem was.

"Are you like this with every female you meet? You know you give off rapey vibes when you act like this." Of course, the mother in me came out, and I tried to explain that he should dial it back if he hoped to find a girl. He left after paying six months of rent as usual, and I didn't have to deal with him for a time.

He occasionally called over the next few months to ask if I had any storage units. He wanted to get one for a guy that worked for him and again later for a vehicle. He asked if I missed him each time and said, "I've been thinking about you. Do you think about me?"

I had gotten to the point where I said mean stuff back to him, like, "Not really." I've told him repeatedly that nothing will happen with us and that he needed to knock it off. I had been very direct with him, but he was like a dog with a bone and would not let it go.

The next time I saw him, he wasn't being so forward or coming onto me. He stood at my counter, paid for storage, and appeared ready to leave. I was relieved and thought he had finally gotten the idea. Then out of the blue, he pulled $1500 out of his wallet and asked me if I would have sex with him for $1500.

I laughed and he said, "I'm not kidding. Right now, take the money and let me have sex with you."

I told him, "You have tried every approach with me, and now you think offering me money like a whore is the way to go about it?" "No, it's not like that at all."

I said, "It's exactly like that. There's no other way to explain it. You are now just treating me like I'm a whore. I'm sure you can find someone to take you up on that offer."

"It's got to be you, though," he said. When he realized that he wasn't getting anywhere, he left. I couldn't believe this guy.

Let's see. I've hit on her, and she has turned me down every time for years; the next best approach would be offering her money like a hooker. That should do the trick. What was he thinking?

The last time I saw him, he upped the offer to $2500, the 'Final offer,' and I declined. He still rents with me, and I'm sure this won't be the last and final offer. I am still trying to figure out what happened in this guy's life that led to him behaving this way.

Part of what brings this on is that I am alone in my office. No one is around to make a guy curb this behavior. I'm a captive audience in my own office. As I mentioned before, I've recently I bought a gun. The pepper spray and billy club were fine but didn't make me feel safe enough. I don't feel quite so vulnerable in my office anymore.

Chapter 4 Thieves

Dad and Son Team

It's incredible what some people will put their kids up to. One day I got to work a little bit earlier than usual, and as always, I took the long way around to my office to check the fence and ensure the facility was clean. As I was coming around the far side of the facility, there was a truck sitting there with a man in the cab. There wasn't any unit door standing open, and he was already in his truck, so I figured he was probably finishing up and leaving. I came around the backside of the facility, and there was a young man I assumed was with the older guy. I could see he had something in his hands, but he turned his back to me and started walking up the aisle. It looked like he had been taking a pee. I parked and went into the office. I looked at the gate controller and saw who it was and how long they had been in. I also checked where his unit was. Sure enough, it was far from where the man had parked his truck. His son was far from where their unit was as well. By the time I had parked and checked the system, they had come up to the gate and keyed their selves out. I walked back to where the boy had been, every single padlock had been cut and turned around not to show the cut. They had been cutting the locks to return later to rob the units.

I called the man, and he answered his phone. I asked him

what had been going on. I wanted to see what story he would give. He asked me what I meant. I asked why he had parked nowhere near his unit and what his son had been doing in the back of the facility. He said his son needed to pee and went back there so no one would see him. Now mind you, I hadn't seen bolt cutters, but the locks were a dead giveaway of what the boy had been doing.

So I said, "So why did your son have bolt cutters with him cutting locks if he was only peeing?" He said, "I didn't know he was doing that. I had no idea. I'm sorry. You aren't going to call the cops, are you? I'll tell him not to do that again. I thought he was peeing."

I said, "I don't think he could have gotten out of your truck with a set of bolt cutters without you noticing."

This kid looked between 14 and 16 years old, and his model father was teaching him to steal. This guy had to be up for Father-Of-The-Year, teaching his son invaluable life skills.

I called the police, but because I hadn't seen the bolt cutters being used on one of the dozen locks that were cut, and they had yet to get into them due to my uncanny timing, they did not get into any trouble. My only recourse was to kick them out of our facility.

Handed To Them On A Silver Platter

Nothing is more frustrating than when a break-in happens. I

take these incidents personally. I always feel like thieves have stolen from my own home. It leaves you feeling violated and usually helpless.

You can have cameras all over the place, giving you an image of a guy or maybe a girl in a black or dark-colored hoodie of average build. It would help if you got the thief to look directly into one of the cameras in broad daylight to tell who they are. It needs to be clear to be used as evidence.

One lovely Summer Saturday, two wonderful scumbags decided to 'go shopping' at one of my storage facilities. It was a girl and guy team. The young man paid his friend $10.00 for the friend's grandmother's gate code. He knew that friend had helped the grandma move in. So, he obtained the code. I was not in that office on the weekend, so they had free reign of the place. They made the rounds and cut off 12 locks. They tore the doors up along the way. They sucked at removing the locks. They had gone in and out of the facility all Saturday morning and afternoon, filling up their car, taking it off-site, and coming back for more. The stuff they took, and there was a lot of it, didn't amount to anything. It was mostly junk. The couple grabbed whatever they could, left with it, and returned for more.

During one of their trips to the storage units, they had the door of one of the units up and they were putting a bunch of used toys and baby items in the back of her car. They took items like old car seats, baby walkers, and toys. They had removed the lock of a long-time customer who ran daycares. The customer that rented the unit two doors down from them happened to come to the facility. He parked, and while getting into his storage unit, he noticed them and recognized them. The female robbing the facility was in drug rehab with the customer's girlfriend. Yeah, I know. But that's not part of this story. He chatted them up and said, "I didn't know you rented here." They played along with it and continued to load the stuff into their car like normal renters. Soon the customer took off, and the thieves finished with that unit. They had been pulling the doors down behind them to avoid drawing attention to what they were doing. When thieves leave the doors ajar, people take notice sooner than when the doors are closed and don't have a lock. They kept this up all afternoon, as I could see that someone had used the code many times to enter and exit. The woman the code belonged to would come in once or twice a year at the most.

The next day, the customer who spoke to them the day before returned to the storage facility and noticed that the locking system and door to his "friend's" storage unit was damaged. Someone had torn the heck out of it getting into it. He called me and explained that they had been there just the previous day, so the break-in must have happened overnight. Unfortunately, it was my only day off, but I decided to head to the storage facility to assess the situation. The customer told me on the phone that he walked down the aisle for a bit and saw that somebody had torn up almost every door in that aisle, and the units had been broken into. I asked him for his friends' names, and he told me. Surprisingly, those individuals were not renters of the unit two doors down from him. I didn't tell him this because I didn't want him to turn tail on me and not want to implicate his friends in the theft. It's possible that he was close to them, and didn't want them to get into trouble.

He explained to me that they had just been there the day before, loading up a bunch of stuff from the storage into their car while talking. I called the police and asked them to meet me at the gate. When the officer pulled up, I told him the guy knew the couple that did the break-ins, but he had no idea those people didn't rent with me and had been robbing the place. I wanted the officer to take his complete statement, and only after implicating these two upstanding citizens would we let him in on what had actually happened there.

The policeman gathered extensive details from the customer, including the items that they were loading into the car and time of day. The policeman was very familiar with the couple due to their frequent involvement in various crimes. The amount of time spent in the facility and the fact that someone used the code a dozen times in one afternoon was pretty damning evidence in and of itself.

To confirm the association, I had called the older woman whose code had been used, and after having the name of the male who did the robbing, she confirmed that her grandson was friends with one of the culprits. I told her what had happened and that if he was a friend of her grandsons, we could be sure he got the code that way. That turned out to be accurate, and she also changed her code.

The officer finished his report, and the customer learned that his "friends" were not renters but thieves. He immediately changed his tone about the two people and expressed that they were acquaintances and that he only knew them because his girlfriend had gone to mandatory drug rehab classes with the girl. He told the policeman he would be happy to help if they needed him again for questioning and seemed sincere about wanting to turn them in once he knew they were stealing from the facility.

I contacted all the customers and compiled a comprehensive list of items stolen from the units, which amounted to well over $5,000 worth of belongings. Many other units were targeted that day, but we assured the victims that we already knew the culprits and had an eyewitness, leading them to believe that justice would prevail. As time passed, I received no updates from the detectives assigned to this case. The case was a slam dunk. We had a witness. And yet, I received nothing. Frustrated, I started giving out the detectives' number to the customers that called in, and I asked them to follow up and see if they had any better luck than I was having.

Purely by chance, I caught one of the detectives at their desk, and my call was put through to them. The detective explained that the eyewitness wasn't cooperating with them. He wasn't giving them the information to bring charges against the couple. She was sorry, but they probably weren't getting anywhere with this. I asked her what more they would need since he gave the first officer their names and what they had taken. It seemed that everything they needed had already been given to them. The longer they waited, the less likely it would be to get any of the stolen goods back to my customers. At this point, I got a little pissed at my customer. If this had been his unit that they robbed, he would have wanted the people caught and charged and maybe even gotten his stolen items back. I decided to call him.

I got him on the phone and immediately asked why he wasn't working with the police. He said he didn't understand what I meant. He had gone to the police department twice already and told them the whole story again. He said they asked him to come down to the station the second time. They asked if he could bring his girlfriend, who had been in mandatory rehab classes with the female thief. He did.

He explained that, during the second visit, the police were not interested in hearing about the storage facility break-ins. They only were interested in the female thief's involvement in package thefts from front porches. Our female thief was known to travel around town and steal packages from porches. She was following around the UPS or Fed-Ex trucks. They knew the female had another female traveling around with her while being a porch pirate. They knew it wasn't my customer's girlfriend but thought she might know the accomplice. Maybe they had talked about it in class. They told the police they had no idea or knowledge of the package thefts but wanted to help with the storage thefts.

They were told that the storage facility theft wasn't a priority. What they wanted to get her on were Federal mail theft charges. In a nutshell, we were screwed. They had bigger fish to fry, and because she had been doing worse stuff they were trying to catch her doing, she was getting a literal "Get out of jail free" pass.

The next time a customer called, I told them the story. I explained them that the witness had given them all the information they needed to bust the thieves; I gave them the names of the thieves and asked them to be sure to call the local police and ask why nothing was going to be done with these two folks.

This situation was incredibly frustrating for several reasons. First, these people were getting off clean and were escaping consequences for their actions. Secondly, it sent a message to other potential thieves that robbing a storage facility is so insignificant you won't even get in trouble even if you are caught.

Lastly, I felt like I was failing my customers by not being able to do a thing to help them. Unfortunately, this wasn't the first time I had handed over criminals to the police only to see no action taken.

Too Ill-Legit to Convict

While I'm on the topic of frustration with catching a thief and the police response, there was a customer who had rented with me for two years without a single issue. He was always prompt with bill payments and hadn't caused any problems. However, one summer, I started experiencing problems with someone breaking into other people's storage units, which were not locked properly.

In our storage facility, to lock a door, you move the latch to the right, similar to a deadbolt, and then put your lock on. If the latch isn't moved to the right, the door can be locked, but it remains open enough for someone to pull it up and access the unit.

The trouble began shortly after I rented a storage unit to a new tenant. Within two days, other customers started reporting issues. Several people had told me that stuff in their storage units had been gone through. The rooms had been rummaged through and moved around enough that they immediately noticed it. I contacted everyone that had left their doors locked in the open position to ask them to return and secure the door as soon as possible.

With 358 units to manage, it was not uncommon for doors to be locked improperly. I instructed people with a mock-up door latch in the office when they first rented with me. Even with the demonstration, people didn't always lock their doors properly.

The problems began immediately following the new tenant renting his storage unit. I started keeping a close eye on him, monitoring his comings and goings and the duration of his stays in the facility. He was new and was moving in and making many trips. So, for now, it wasn't anything unusual. I started to notice that every time there was an incident, he and this long-time customer had both been in. Not necessarily at the same time, but both had been in around the time of each robbery. Several others had also been in, and I was trying to triangulate all this information and narrow it down to one person. This process relied on customers reporting issues to me.

A few days later, an entire couch and some furniture were stolen. We are talking about some pretty big furniture. This was a devastating loss for a young girl who had her whole storage unit full of brand-new items, gifted to her by family members for her upcoming graduation. She was about to move into a place of her own as well. Somebody had taken all of it overnight. She had come to put some additional items in her storage unit and left the door improperly latched. When I got to work the next day and noticed that she had locked it in an open position, it was too late. This was getting worse.

The beautiful weather and frequent customer traffic made it challenging for me to narrow down who it was. I still managed to narrow it down to two people and was 98 percent sure it was one of them. Then, a breakthrough came when a doctor who stored vintage camera gear suddenly realized he had not locked his door right.

He hurried back to the facility, only to find that 80% of it was gone. They had quickly loaded up his unit and left with the contents. When he returned to check his door, no one else was in the facility. He called me right away and told me what had just happened. I was at my other office at the time. I got on the computer and saw that one of the two people I suspected had been the only person to have keyed themselves in when the Doctor had come and gone. Only about half an hour had elapsed, but it was enough time for the bad guy to make his daily trip around the facility looking for locked open doors, clean out the unit and leave again. I had no video footage of this, and my video of his truck was inconclusive because it had a Leer cap on it, and you couldn't see what was inside. But he was the only person in there, and there was one more piece of damning evidence.

This long-time customer had always used a crutch to get around—just one. It was an aluminum crutch with a rag wrapped around the top of it to cushion under his armpit. The material looked like it should have been changed a few years ago. He had come to the office the day before to make his monthly payment and was, at that time, still using that crutch. He once told me that he was disabled and couldn't work, but I sometimes saw him get out of the truck without using the crutch. I would also see him prop it against his vehicle whenever he wanted to move something big in or out of his storage unit. Perhaps he was having a good day at those moments and wasn't in too much pain.

On this particular day, he must have been having a super good day because not only was he able to load doctor's storage unit up in record time, he must not have needed his crutch much because he left it in doctor's storage unit. Doctor told me this when he called, and I asked him if he had touched or moved anything. He explained that he had just shut the door and locked it correctly with the crutch still leaning against the wall inside his unit. I told him I knew who his thief was and that we would take care of this. I promptly called the police and informed them about the situation.

The officer showed up, and doctor provided a list of stolen items from the unit. I showed the officer where this long-time customer had been in the facility every single time something had come up missing; this time, he was the ONLY person that had been in when the theft happened.

In addition, we had his crutch that he had left behind in the storage unit. He didn't need the crutch as much as he would let others believe. The officer took the crutch back to the station as evidence, along with our reports. I felt relieved that I had finally caught the thief and hoped this would put an end to his stealing spree at my facility.

The very next day, the police arrived with a warrant. We cut off the perpetrator's lock, and they searched for stolen items. Based on people's descriptions, none of the stolen merchandise was in his unit. He was taking it elsewhere and not dropping it off in his storage. That would make sense as he was coming and going so quickly between each robbery. He wasn't taking the chance of getting caught red-handed with the stolen goods.

While the police were taking pictures of the things in his unit, he showed up at the storage facility. I was earlier than usual, because I was there to meet with the officers. He opened the gate, came in, and pulled into the row where his storage unit was. Upon seeing the police officers inside, an innocent person would get out and ask what was happening. He would ask why all these people were in his storage unit. But nope, he saw what was going on and backed up, and quickly left the premises, using his access code to exit. He knew he had been busted. There was no other explanation for why he would see what was happening and immediately leave without question. I watched him go, and I walked out and told the police that the guy that just pulled in, backed up, and left was the guy whose unit they were going through. Even the police officers said, "That's the actions of a guilty party." They found no stolen items in his storage unit, but we had enough evidence against him anyway.

I called the perpetrator and told him he was being evicted. His access code was restricted to the hours when I would be on the premises, and he had 24 hours to vacate. He never once asked me why. He simply stated that he had to wait until the following day. The next day he showed up, cleaned out his storage unit, and left. He knew precisely why he was asked to leave. Again, this would be the behavior of a guilty person. If I had done nothing wrong, I would have been asking a few questions. I would wonder what was going on. He left without incident, and we awaited his day in court.

Charges were filed against him, and he appeared before the judge. The responding officer was there as well. He came into court hobbling like he was half-paralyzed, using a crutch as if it were the only way he could get around. He was putting on the biggest show possible. The judge told him what he had been charged with, and he explained to the judge that he couldn't have possibly done what he was being accused of, claiming that he could hardly walk. He explained how he had been unable to work because of his disability and pain. The judge dismissed the charges, believing that it would be impossible for someone in his condition to have stolen the items and gotten them into his truck when he was barely able to walk. With the size of some of the items stolen, it just wasn't possible. With him being in the facility every time something happened, being the only person in when the doctor was robbed, and even leaving his crutch behind in the storage unit, he walked. Well, he hobbled anyway. I couldn't believe it! Here was another case in which the judge was handed a thief on a silver platter, and he got away with it. There must be a 'Get Out Of Jail Free Card' for anyone robbing storage units. It felt disheartening, especially for the customers who had been victimized. They must have felt even more helpless than I did.

Adding to the frustration, this same customer had the audacity to return about a year later and ask if he could another storage unit. Needless to say, I turned him away without hesitation.

Chapter 5 Angry Customers

The Church Lady

Every once in a while, a customer leaves an indelible impression. This lady is one such customer. From the outset, she made her presence felt. Initially, she was a typical late-paying customer: falling behind by one or two months, then settling her debt in full, only to fall behind again shortly after. Her tendency to brag was notable. She'd often boast about her recent windfalls, leaving me puzzled as to why she couldn't settle her bill on time. Each month, she'd conjure up an elaborate excuse for her delay, and this would persist until she eventually cleared her dues. During her early days, she never allowed the debt to surpass two months before paying.

About a year into her rental agreement, she started pushing boundaries further, edging towards auction territory. By Indiana law, when a unit's payment is 30 days overdue, a late notice is sent. At 60 days, the tenant receives an auction notice specifying the date of the unit's auction, which can commence on the 91st day of delinquency or later. This lengthy procedure, filled with paperwork, calls, and legal notices in local newspapers (costing around $135.00 per ad), is tedious and costly for storage facilities. Rarely do we break even, given that many of the abandoned storage contents are worthless. While there might be one or two valuable items occasionally, most of the contents could be discarded without much fuss.

Indiana's lien laws heavily favor the tenant over the facility owner. This woman's unit was consistently on the brink of auction every three months. She would invariably dispute her bill upon receiving the auction notice. Her monthly bill, coupled with a $10.00 late fee posted the 7th of each month, was straightforward, yet she felt compelled to argue about it. Soon after, she'd inquire about partial payments.

To clarify the situation, I'd dispatch a comprehensible letter alongside the auction notice. This letter explicitly stated that unless the full payment was made by a specific date, we'd be forced to auction the unit's contents. It highlighted that partial payments at this late stage were unacceptable, as it would set a precedent for chronic delinquency. This letter also made it clear that only cash, card, or money orders were acceptable forms of payment, no checks. Yet, like clockwork, she'd assert her desire for a partial payment. Even after explaining that partial payments were viable only in the early stages of delinquency and not after accruing ad expenses, she'd react vehemently. She'd threaten legal action and demand that I furnish a law barring partial payments. While our refusal policy was stated explicitly on our contract's front page, she persisted. After one too many confrontations, I challenged her to produce a law that obliged me to accept partial payments. Her recurrent calls became a source of dread for me.

Invariably, she'd clear her dues just before an auction, often moments before, all the while maintaining an acrimonious demeanor.

Toward the end of our association, her behavior escalated. After her routine threat of suing over the partial payment refusal, she'd call, demanding an itemized monthly bill highlighting the late fees. It seemed nothing more than a stalling tactic, causing undue stress and work on my part. I doubted she ever reviewed the emailed documents; it was merely a power play. She frequently mentioned impending settlement checks and even claimed to have studied law. However, studying law and perpetually threatening lawsuits are entirely different endeavors. Her life seemed a patchwork of settlement checks interspersed with disability payments. Her specific disability remains a mystery to me, or perhaps, it just slipped my mind.

The last time her unit was up for auction, she phoned to inquire about her outstanding balance. As always, she demanded a meticulous breakdown of the charges, item by item. Although these charges were consistent, she pressed for details. Unexpectedly, she claimed that auctioning the unit would be unacceptable since some of its contents belonged to her church, presumably the one she attended. I wasn't sure why she had stored church items for years, but that wasn't my concern. I clarified that unless it was a vehicle or item with another lien, the contents would be auctioned off if payment wasn't settled. Her reaction was explosive. She accused me of being "evil," claimed I was cursed with illness due to my supposedly malevolent heart (despite me not being ill), and then resorted to hurling profanities. The intensity of her screaming was so pronounced that my husband, from across the room, could hear her outburst. I calmly pointed out the irony of her behavior, given her insistence that some items in storage were from her church. She promptly hung up.

Unexpectedly, she called back later to ask how the storage unit could be transferred from her daughter's name to hers. When she initially rented the unit, it was under her daughter's name, which I suspected was a strategy to sidestep previous debts, possibly even to other facilities. Given that her daughter was around 19 when they first visited, this seemed plausible. I explained the procedure: both of them had to visit the office, where the daughter would relinquish her rights to the unit and the mother would complete a new contract. In due course, both complied with this request.

However, a twist awaited. A mere two days later, she announced that her attorney had sent me her bankruptcy documentation. The timing wasn't coincidental; the auction was slated for two days later. She had cleverly manipulated the situation to her advantage. Now, with her declaring bankruptcy, I couldn't auction the unit. I would need to assess the content's value, contrast it with her outstanding balance, and liaise with the courts. I was anticipating this unit's auction and finally parting ways with this taxing customer.

Leveraging the insufficient notice of her bankruptcy—only two days prior—I decided to evict her. Evictions typically provide tenants with a deadline to vacate, after which any remaining belongings are no longer their property. However, such situations seldom proceed smoothly. From experience, tenants either miss their deadlines, leave junk behind, or both. Over the course of 18 years, I've never managed a seamless eviction. Predictably, this instance was chaotic. She overstayed her deadline by a week. Since her access code was deactivated due to delinquency, I had to manually let her in during every visit. As expected, she left behind rubbish: a decrepit couch, broken furniture pieces, and a heap of trash sufficient to fill a contractor's bag. Nonetheless, she was finally out of my hair. All in all, it still felt like a victory.

Mother-In-Laws China

One of my significant pet peeves is being inadvertently involved in domestic disputes. Over the years, I've encountered countless couples who have rented from me and subsequently parted ways while still leasing storage. Some covertly stash items from shared homes, sometimes in the midst of purchasing new furnishings for a yet-to-be-revealed residence. Often, they fund these endeavors using their unsuspecting partner's money. In other instances, after heated disagreements, one partner seeks storage for their possessions. However, these separations tend to be short-lived, and the items are often retrieved within weeks upon reconciliation. It's challenging not to sympathize with one party over the other, especially when one adopts a confrontational stance, implicating me in their domestic feud.

On one occasion, a genial young man, probably in his late twenties, rented a 10 x 10 unit near the facility's entrance, easily visible from the road and to the adjacent neighbor.

A week later, the same neighbor called, informing me that a woman wielding a hammer was attempting to break a storage unit's lock. The neighbor had already informed the sheriff. By the time I reached the site, the woman had fled, evading both me and the arriving police officers. As described, the storage unit's door bore evidence of her aggressive lock-picking attempt, though she hadn't succeeded in accessing the unit. I contacted the tenant, sharing the woman's description. Without hesitation, he identified her as his estranged wife. Evidently, she had discovered his storage location through mutual acquaintances and, by observing him, had deduced his unit number. Without his access code, she had craftily rented her own space to enter the facility, subsequently targeting his unit. He expressed his regret for the commotion and assured me he would address the matter with her. Checking her rented unit, I found it predictably empty. I then informed her of the termination of her rental agreement, the reasons being her prior misconduct. Graciously, I refrained from pressing charges, settling only for repairing the slightly damaged latch.

Her response was a vehement visit to my office the following day, demanding access to her husband's unit. I calmly explained the stipulations of the lease agreement, which permitted access solely to the signatory – her husband. Outraged, she threatened legal action, claiming a right to the unit's contents as his wife. I pondered the urgency of her claim – was the storage unit a cache of essentials that he'd removed from their shared home? Regardless, I reiterated the legal channels she should follow if her allegations held merit.

Undeterred, she returned the next day, this time accompanied by her mother. Their tandem assault of vociferous demands continued, asserting that I was obstructing them from retrieving their belongings. Reiterating my stance for the umpteenth time, I was met with an accusatory insinuation of a personal relationship with the husband. My patience having worn thin, I sternly directed them to leave with a warning of impending police involvement. Fortunately, they heeded the caution, but their combined hostility left me apprehensive of potential physical threats.

I despise confrontation. I often sidestep it, even if it means being trampled over. My body reacts instantaneously – trembling hands, a parched mouth, and a dizzying sensation. While I maintain composure outwardly, internally, it's a whirlwind. Once the situation dissipates and I'm alone, I need a few moments to gather myself, and this was one such instance.

I contacted the young man renting the storage unit, informing him about his wife's return and her mother's accompanying presence. I subtly suggested relocating his belongings, given the incessant disturbances. That's when he revealed the root of the contention. Contrary to her claims, the storage contained nothing belonging to his estranged wife. Their assets had been legally divided in court, with each item he possessed clearly listed in the divorce agreement.

"You or any police officer can inspect the contents. They're all documented," he assured. Out of their decade-long union, he'd retained merely eight possessions. Thankfully, they had no children in the mix. He confessed to prioritizing peace over material gains. Opting to leave with only what he'd brought into the marriage, he vacated the majority of their shared belongings. His main treasure? A china set, once his late mother's.

"It's my sole keepsake from her time," he shared.

The china's intrinsic value wasn't financial but sentimental. Grasping the depth of their dispute over this heirloom stunned me. His wife's extreme reactions were ostensibly driven by an irrational obsession over this set.

Yet, she had one more stratagem up her sleeve. This time, she dispatched her father. Contrary to the emotional volatility exhibited by his daughter and wife, he approached the matter with quietude. After I reiterated the contractual stipulations that barred unauthorized access, he simply nodded, acknowledging my stance, and departed. That was the conclusion of my interactions with that family. Days later, the young tenant informed me of his decision to shift his belongings to an undisclosed location in the interests of all parties.

While I recognize the heightened emotions accompanying separations, the consistent pattern of being involuntarily thrust into these disputes frustrates me. Being roped in as a mediator isn't within my job description.

Taking His Side

Domestic disputes are often the most challenging situations storage operators like myself, have to navigate. One such incident remains vivid in my memory.

I had a couple who had been tenants for several years. They rented multiple storage units from me. Both the husband and wife frequently interacted with me, either in person or over the phone. Although I spoke to both, I conversed with the wife more frequently. One day, she visited, tearfully revealing that her husband was divorcing her. Initially, she was heartbroken, fearing financial instability and potential homelessness, especially since her name wasn't on their house deed. The house had been his prior to their marriage, which spanned roughly 10 to 15 years. Surprisingly, post-divorce, he was slated to retain it. While this might seem fair to some, given Indiana's property laws, I wouldn't have been taken aback if the court had decided otherwise. She was granted a deadline to evacuate her belongings from their shared residence. Unfortunately, this deadline had passed, and she hadn't acted. Considering both were retired, I chalked this delay up to simple procrastination.

Eventually, she approached me, seeking a new storage unit separate from the ones she previously shared with her husband. This unit was to house items from their home and the assets she was awarded during their court proceedings. I complied, and she returned with her family to store her belongings. Days later, she phoned me, distraught as usual, demanding I sever the locks on the old units to retrieve her items. Every call was a roller-coaster, with her oscillating between heartbreak over the loss of her marital security and fury towards her estranged husband. As she vented her frustrations, regaling me with the intricate details of their marital discord, our conversations would inevitably meander. My primary objective was to ascertain her permission to cut the locks. Despite being the primary name on the storage agreement, with her husband as a secondary, she hesitated in granting me straightforward approval.

It took a draining 20 minutes before I could suggest a potential solution: cutting the locks and replacing them, with the expenses billed to her. This proposal further incensed her, leading to accusations of my insensitivity. I genuinely believed I was offering an empathetic ear, enduring these lengthy, emotional calls. Yet, her demands took a toll on my daily productivity. Towards the conclusion of our conversation, she revealed a crucial piece of information: they were still in the midst of property division negotiations. The court had apparently advised her against making any rash decisions. My suggestion, then, was for her to obtain the keys from her ex-husband through their lawyers, eliminating any direct confrontations and ensuring I remained impartial. This, however, sparked another outburst, as she accused me of siding with her husband. I tried assuring her of my neutrality, but it took considerable effort to placate her and conclude the call.

The next day, she phoned again, inquiring if her ex had reached out to me. She had texted him, asking him to deliver the keys to me. When I informed her he hadn't, she pressed me to call him. I reiterated my reluctance to intervene. She then revealed she'd added another set of locks on the units, distrusting him enough to believe he might prematurely remove items, especially given their ongoing legal discussions regarding property division. With their disagreements extending to even the minutest of possessions and given her constant calls to me, I wasn't surprised by the contention. From experience, I knew it was usually the more vocal party that posed the greater challenge.

Later that day, the soon-to-be ex-husband rang. Apologizing for dragging me into their mess, he candidly expressed his frustration with her, labeling her as unhinged. He promised to drop off the keys the next morning, emphasizing his indifference to the contents of the storage and his eagerness for closure. She subsequently called, ensuring I would remove his locks upon receipt of the keys and reach out once done.

The following day, he visited, his appearance startlingly indicative of extreme stress. Apologetically, he shared that while he originally sought his tools from storage, he'd relinquished all claims that morning. Offering to return his locks, he declined, preferring to sever all ties to the tumultuous situation. I obliged, removed his locks, and informed her. Predictably, she called right after, probing about our conversation. On mentioning the discarded locks, she was incensed, demanding their reinstatement and his return for the keys. Firmly, I declined, suggesting she either use the locks herself or discard them, but reiterated I wouldn't be playing a game of lock-switching based on her whims.

Drained after another half-hour call, during which she predictably revisited every alleged grievance against her ex, she leveled a shocking accusation: she believed I was having an affair with her husband purely because I wasn't vilifying him at her behest. She further insisted on visiting my office for a face-to-face talk, which I firmly declined.

Indeed, he was accurate in his assessment of her volatile nature. Ironically, after all the fuss, I reinstalled the locks, and she only claimed the keys a month later.

The saga with this woman extended for several more months. Various family members reached out to me, one of whom had asked her to leave his home. He had graciously allowed her to stay with him following her split from her husband, but that arrangement lasted less than a month. Unable to cope with her behavior, he requested she find another place. She subsequently moved in with one of her children, who had never been fond of the husband. Bonding over their mutual disdain for the ex, they provided her with a more amicable living arrangement. To my knowledge, she remains with them to this day.

Four months later, she decided to move out, emptying all the storage units. Over time, she had distributed his belongings to friends and family, taking immense pride in her actions. Not only did she not want any of his possessions, but she was also determined that he shouldn't reclaim any of them. She proclaimed greater satisfaction in giving everything away than in allowing him to recover his belongings. However, she indicated she would be leaving a few items she no longer wanted. I emphasized the need for her to remove everything, as I didn't have the means to dispose of large items.

"It's just some box springs and mattresses," she replied.

Unfortunately, those were the very items I couldn't easily dispose of, even at the local dump. Her tears emerged once more, and she lamented about me "taking his side" again. I clarified that my request to remove all belongings was independent of her relationship with her ex, reminding her that retention of her security deposit hinged on her compliance. While I understand that divorces can be tumultuous and that emotions run high, this particular situation was extraordinarily challenging. The day she vacated the premises was a day of immense relief for me. On a concluding note, she did, in the end, take those old mattresses with her.

Are You Sleeping With My Husband?

I recently asked someone if I come off as promiscuous. For most of my adult life, I've been slightly overweight, a challenge I've grappled with intermittently. I rarely wear makeup, and my go-to outfits consist of oversized sweatshirts paired with worn jeans during the winter. On days I feel particularly bloated, I opt for sweatpants. Summer attire is an oversized t-shirt and knee-length shorts. My style can be likened to that of a middle-aged lesbian. Sometimes, I get so caught up in my routine that I forget to shave my legs until sunlight reveals its ape-like texture. Given all this, why am I often wrongly accused of being involved with someone's husband? Most times, I haven't even had a conversation with the man in question. On some occasions, I feel indignant. I'd like to think I have better standards and might even be out of the league of the husband I'm accused of being with. I want to exclaim, "Really? Have you taken a good look at your husband?" But then, beauty is subjective.

I once had a customer who rented from me for about five years. He eventually got married, and although I had never met his wife, she'd called a few times to handle the rent payments. Our interactions over the phone were always amicable and uneventful. Then one day, out of nowhere, she asked pointedly, "Ginger, have you been involved with my husband?" This caught me off guard. I hadn't seen her husband for months, and our interactions, when he used to visit, were always brief and professional. I clarified that there was no truth to her suspicion and tried to understand where it was stemming from. She admitted she hadn't found any evidence but just had a "feeling." If her intuition was on point, it certainly had nothing to do with me.

A few months later, the man's parents visited my office to handle his monthly payment since he was out of town. His mother shared that he and his wife were divorcing because the latter was "somewhat unhinged." She elaborated on how the wife had been reaching out to multiple acquaintances, accusing them of being involved with her husband. I played along, pretending to be shocked, even though I had been on the receiving end of one such call. His mother emphasized that her son was honorable and felt he had been pushed away by his wife's unfounded insecurities. I kind of saw that coming to be honest.

Thank Goodness for Walter

It was a beautiful late Spring day. After an auction, a few buyers were still clearing out their units. I drove by one unit and briefly spoke with some of the purchasers as they sorted and loaded their newfound belongings. Halley, one of our regular buyers, was struggling with a gas grill. Noting its weight, he opened its bottom doors, expecting a full propane tank. Instead, we found a petite casket used for cremains. Inside was a bag of ashes. It was shocking that someone would abandon a storage unit, especially leaving a loved one's remains behind. I transported the casket to my golf cart, and "Walter" found a temporary resting place on a shelf in my office.

After some online research, I learned that a tag inside would indicate the funeral home. It seemed like the best lead, especially since my attempts to contact the unit's owner had failed—no phone connection and letters returned undeliverable

Jokingly, I was at a "dead" end and had to think outside the "box."

When I reached out to the local funeral home on the tag, they instantly recognized the woman's name. Relaying the situation to the funeral director, he recalled the woman being distressed over receiving her husband's remains in a simple box. In sympathy, he had provided her with a floor model casket at no cost. Sadly, he didn't have updated contact information for her or knowledge of any living relatives. Walter sat on my office shelf for about a month. Unexpectedly, the elusive customer walked in one day. She was quite tall, and accompanied by two women of similar stature, stood defensively. Their demeanor suggested they were ready for confrontation. Admittedly, I felt vulnerable, given my age and health.

"Why did you sell my storage unit?" she began. I calmly clarified that the unit was sold due to months of non-payment, which is standard procedure after three months of default. She angrily questioned why I hadn't informed her. When I provided her with the address and phone number on record, she retorted that she had updated her information. However, our KIOSK records proved otherwise.

Her frustration grew as her accusations unraveled. With heightened emotion, she moved around the counter, closing the distance between us. Panic set in. I imagined the worst scenarios from every brawling video I'd seen online. At 50, it seemed I was about to face my first physical confrontation, and the odds weren't in my favor.

Suddenly, I blurted out, "Hey, hey, can I ask you something real quick?" She halted, staring intently, perhaps anticipating an offer of compensation.

"Did you recently lose a pet?" I inquired.

Confused, she responded, "What?"

I pressed on, "Did you recently lose a pet? I found some cremains in the storage unit. Given their placement at the bottom of a gas grill, I assumed they might belong to a dog or cat."

Her companion on the left, evidently recognizing the implication, exclaimed in disbelief, "Did you store Walter in there? Why was he in the bottom of a gas grill?" Instantly, the tables turned. The main aggressor now faced the wrath of her backup. The other woman, silent till now, took a step back, clearly uncomfortable.

It transpired that "Walter" was her brother, making the woman his sister-in-law. She was mortified that her brother's remains were abandoned in such a manner. Seizing the moment, I assured her, "It's okay. Fortunately, we discovered his remains during the unit's clearance. I've kept them safe in the back, awaiting someone to claim him. I even reached out to the funeral home, but they didn't have any updated contact details."

"Thank God he wasn't discarded. I can't believe you did this," the sister-in-law rebuked the main woman, firmly stating she would take her brother's remains. We loaded Walter onto a dolly, wheeled him to her car's trunk, and soon after, the trio departed, never to contact me again.

I'm still amazed at how the off-the-cuff "pet in the grill" comment played out. While I might lack physical height, I clearly possess the ability to think swiftly in tense situations.

Chapter 6 Just Plain Weird Stuff

Dildo Storage Wars

I was fairly new to the storage auction scene, having only managed two or three sales at that point. Curious about the process, the owner of the storage facility decided to attend one of the auctions. It turned out to be the only one he'd ever attend. On auction day, with fantastic weather and a good turnout, familiar faces from previous sales were present. Just like on the TV show "Storage Wars," there are always a few attendees who don't get along and a couple who enjoy the playful banter and teasing.

We began with the first unit. Contrary to what's shown on TV, the locks on our units for auction are already removed and replaced with site-owned ones. Upon lifting the door, the contents can be viewed without entering. To everyone's astonishment, the first item we saw was a large, anatomically correct penis-shaped piggy bank standing about 3.5 feet tall. Everyone noticed it, and naturally, my boisterous crowd couldn't let it pass without comment. The teasing began, especially towards one regular attendee who, they joked, would surely bid higher for the unit due to the unique bank. After some spirited bidding, the unit was sold, and we moved on.

The subsequent unit, owned by a different individual and just a few steps away, had another surprise in store. The door went up to reveal a laundry basket of linens, and prominently displayed on top was an extraordinarily large, veiny dildo, complete with a suction cup at the base. Given this was the second phallic discovery in a row, the crowd was now even more animated. Some teased that I had orchestrated this intentionally, though I assuredly had not. In my 18 years in the business, I had never come across such items, especially not in consecutive units.

My primary concern was what my boss, attending his first auction, would think. Of all the auctions for him to witness, why did it have to be this one?

Unbelievably, the third unit continued the trend. It appeared typical, filled with household items, furniture, and an array of boxes and totes. But prominently displayed on a metal shelf were two more dildos. The baffling coincidence of these finds, especially considering the units weren't owned by the same individuals, was beyond explanation. Strangely, I hadn't noticed these items when initially cutting the locks. By this point, the owner had seen enough. He shook his head, turned, and left, never to attend another auction again.

Though several other units were auctioned off that day, the bizarre trend concluded with that third unit. There have been no such discoveries since that singularly strange storage auction day.

Hoarders

In my line of work, I've encountered many hoarders, but two particular cases stand out. The first involved a woman who eventually lost her possessions to an auction, and the second centered around a man who passed away, leaving a caregiver to clear out his units.

Let's delve into the story of the woman first. I hesitate to use the term "lady" when referring to her, especially after witnessing her engage in a near-physical altercation outside the office with another customer. The profanities she spewed would have easily shocked the most seasoned sailor. I'll admit to occasionally using strong language, but her words were in a league of their own. This particular incident with her is detailed in another chapter of this book, but her notoriety merits a mention here as well. Initially, she rented a single storage unit, but in a span of a few weeks, she expanded to five of our largest units, each measuring 10 ft x 30 ft. Additionally, she occupied a couple of 10 ft x 15 ft units, which she settled for when our larger units were fully booked. I never saw her arrive with a truck; she always seemed to unload items from the back seat, passenger seat, and trunk of her car. After unloading, she'd promptly leave, only to return shortly with another batch of items. This cycle often ended with her renting another unit. For about a year, she made regular monthly payments via credit card. However, problems arose when her card was either maxed out or possibly deactivated due to non-payment.

She came into the office only once after the payments began to back up. She had gotten her first late notice, and it was heading to the auction notice stage. She didn't appear upset and asked me, "What would happen if she couldn't pay the bill?" That was the last time I saw her. I attempted to call her a few times to see what was happening because seven storage units packed to the gills were a lot to walk away from, but this is what she had done. The weeks passed, and we were down to just five days before the auction. I hadn't taken her locks off yet in hopes that she would come up with the money, but we were well over a thousand dollars then, and I knew she wouldn't be able to. I began to cut off the locks and was shocked at how much stuff she had packed into these units. They were filled to the ceilings. The back of the units had 15-foot tall ceilings at their peak and 10 feet towards the front. When you opened the doors, it all came down like a landslide. She was organized about which unit held the bulk of any given item, but the way they were filled was anything but organized. Things had been thrown in there, one on top of the next.

Some of the units were just full of clothing and "hooker shoes." I say "hooker shoes" because these were not practical shoes unless you were hooking or clubbing. These were the highest of high heels, rivaling the stiletto. Tons of gems, sequins, and be-dazzling adorned all the shoes and boots. The clothing was about the same. If this woman was about to start the world's largest prostitution empire, she could easily keep all the girls in clothing for years. She might have liked the clothing for herself, but I never saw her dress like that, and she was in her sixties at least. Other units contained household items—countertop appliances, dishes, glassware, and anything you might use in the kitchen.

Most of these items had the tags on or were still in the store packaging. We noticed that a few of the things had come from thrift stores and yard sales as well. So, she was an equal-opportunity buyer.

When the day came for the auction, we did well in recouping our losses on the units. I had to give the people who purchased the units extra time to empty them. They were packed so full that each took over a week to empty.

I have yet to hear from her again. After she came in initially and asked what would happen to her stuff, she never came back or called.

I recently spoke with one of the buyers from that day, and after several years, they are still selling off the stuff that came out of the unit they bought.

My second hoarder was more of the typical type on the popular TV show, but he was super organized about it. He had four storage units. He was super good about paying his monthly bill, but he passed away. A caregiver came in on his behalf to clean out his storage units. One of the units had a few collectibles and antiques. Those items were the things that the customer thought was of high value and needed to be in a unit of their own. When it was all said and done, the person who cleared the units out for him ended up with two salvageable desks, perhaps worth selling. On top of the desks were some political pins, medals, and other small antique items that would be valuable to a collector. Everything in that unit that was worth keeping and not hauling off to the dump fit on the top of these two small writing desks. He laid out the items nicely on display and, after posting pictures of the things online, found a buyer after about a week. The caregiver then asked me if it would be okay to rent a dumpster to clean out the rest of the units. I thought he meant one of the smaller ones you see behind stores. Instead, it was a full-length dumpster, and he barely had enough room to get everything in. Here in our city, if you want to recycle anything, it will cost you. If it needs to be picked up, there will be additional charges. So, there is probably little recycling going on here. Two of this man's rented units could have been 100% recyclable. In fact, that was his original intention, but he found that it would cost him dearly to get the items recycled.

One unit was filled top to bottom with newspapers. Not unique articles or editions containing memorable moments in history. Just everyday newspapers that he had bundled up with twine were stacked ceiling to floor in the storage unit. The next unit was filled with plastic drinking bottles and again filled from top to bottom solid with bottles. The dumpster was too big to bring inside the storage facility, so they spent days and days filling up pick-up trucks and taking them to the dumpster just outside the gate. I never did find out what was in the fourth storage unit, but I know that the entire contents went to the dump after it was gone through. This man had been paying for this storage for many years. He was a customer that we "inherited" from the previous owner of that particular facility. His original intentions were good ones. He was going to help the Earth by recycling all that paper and plastic, and either it got away from him, or he found that it was just too expensive to accomplish. Another unit was full of trash. His final unit contained two desks and a handful of items of value. I am sure that in his mind, though, it all had value, one way or another.

Every time there is a dumpster that the public can access, divers are nearby. These divers were disappointed when they found that over 99% of the dumpster contained trash, plastic bottles, and newspapers.

Live In Guest

I often get asked if people try to live in storage units. Fortunately, in the 18 years, I've been in this business, it hasn't been a significant issue. If I notice that someone hasn't exited after hours, I typically call them and remind them to leave by 9

PM or warn them that I'll have to call the sheriff or police. This usually resolves the matter immediately, as many of these individuals have had past run-ins with the law and want to avoid any further encounters.

Recently, I noticed someone in the facility after hours. I sent the sheriff to check on the situation, providing them with the gate code so they could access the premises and "surprise" any potential wrongdoers. Upon arrival, the police found a truck parked inside with our customer unresponsive at the wheel due to an overdose. Thankfully, they managed to revive her, sending her to the hospital via ambulance while her truck was towed away. I sometimes wonder if I would have found her in a worse state the next day if they hadn't intervened. She never broached the topic with me, and I never inquired further. A few months later, after consistently being late with her payments, she vacated one of her units—leaving behind a small amount of debris in one and a plethora of broken items in the other. It's intriguing that customers often realize upon moving out that they've stored unnecessary items, yet they seldom have this insight when initially moving in.

In another incident, upon arriving at my second office for the day, I noticed a long orange extension cord snaking across the parking lot, plugged into a light post. Approaching it, I found the cord hot to touch, leading me to disconnect it swiftly and trace it back to its source—a storage unit. Without a lock barring entry, I quickly lifted the door to discover three young adults inside, shrouded in a thick layer of cigarette smoke. Amidst blankets and sleeping bags, they were utilizing a space heater with a sizeable ash pile as evidence of their chain smoking. The sudden intrusion likely startled them, but I calmly informed them that they had to vacate the premises immediately, assuring them that I wouldn't involve the authorities. Gratefully, they complied. The primary tenant had only rented the space the previous afternoon; their stay with us lasted merely a night.

Upon their departure, I promptly closed out their account and deactivated their gate code to prevent reentry. Later that day, I returned to clean the unit and found they had left behind blankets, sleeping bags, and the extension cord. After storing these items in the garage for a couple of weeks without anyone returning to claim them, I decided to make use of the space heater and extension cord—they've proven useful over time.

What the hell? Are you two years old?

When COVID hit, I worked from home during March and April. I returned on the first of May. Luckily, the weather had been pretty cooperative, and so far, no one had been around any time it rained or the temperature was frigid. I kept a fold-up utility table right outside my office door with a fold-up chair where people could fill out their rental paperwork. This way, I didn't have to close down due to Covid-19 and could still care for the customers. I would spray the table with Lysol and clean the pen for the next person. I always wore a mask when caring for the customers and asked them to wear one too. During this time, the news claimed that half the population would die from COVID-19. Everything was up in the air, and I didn't want to take any chances.

I got a new customer the first day I was back in the office. When this particular customer first walked up to the gate to come to do the paperwork for his rental, I saw that he wasn't wearing a mask and was coughing as if he had tuberculosis. His cough was super concerning to me. He just kept hacking, and I almost asked if the guy that came with him could do the paperwork instead. His friend wasn't hacking and coughing; I would have felt better. He reluctantly returned to his vehicle and got a mask; his friend did as well. Neither intended to wear a mask and weren't happy I asked them to. I explained to them that I had Lupus and that wearing a mask was not a choice. He came up to the table, grumbled something under his breath, plopped down on the folding chair, and began filling out the paperwork. He pulled the mask down under his chin, and I stepped back. He was still coughing and spewing spit and phlegm everywhere. I stepped back a few steps and asked if he wouldn't mind putting the mask back over his mouth and nose. He did it for a moment, then pulled it back down again. His friend kept stepping up to the table and speaking with him, and he lowered his mask below his chin every time he stepped forward. I was beginning to realize they were doing this on purpose because they were upset that I would ask them to wear the masks in the first place. The bad attitude coming from both of them was obvious. I just wanted to hurry up and get the paperwork done, and every time I stepped up to the table where he was sitting, I would try to hold my breath. We got his paperwork done, and he was on his way. I took extra care not to touch my face, eyes, or mouth and washed up with soap and water after taking care of them, just in case.

Just a few days later, I was getting ready to go home. I was walking out to my car to put some items in before I closed up for the day. It was about 4:58, and we closed at 5:00 pm. Someone had just pulled up to the gate. I assumed they were coming in to go to their storage unit this late in the day. Instead, he yells at me, "Hey, open this gate!" I don't recognize who it is and ask him if he has a code for the gate. He replies that he does, but he doesn't remember it. Now, I need to check to ensure that this person rents here and has paid his bill. I tell him I will unlock the walk-in gate to the side of the full-sized drive-through gate and give the code to him. I tell him I am getting ready to leave, and if he doesn't have his code, he will be locked in. He yells at me again, "Just open the gate!"

I hit the gate release button that activates a magnetic door latch so he can enter the walk-through gate on foot. I stand at my office door, which currently has a white folding utility table in front of it and the chair. I asked for his name, and instantly I realized who he was. He is, once again, not wearing a mask. He asks me if he can use my bathroom. I told him that because of Covid-19, no one is allowed in the office. I don't have the means of cleaning it properly after each customer, besides the fact that the guy has come to my office again with no mask on. It's only been a few days since he rented, and after, I had to ask him to put his mask back up several times. In addition, the table and chair are still blocking the door with a sign asking them to wait there for service. I think he already knew the answer to his question. I apologized for him not being able to come into the office and told him I'd be right back with his gate code. I am talking with him, telling him I want to write his code down because I am leaving right now and don't want him to be locked in. I note his gate code on a business card and walk back to the door. He is standing there, pissing down his leg. His jeans are soaked. He is standing on one leg, and as the pee accumulates on his shoe, he is flicking it off his leg and shoe in the direction of my door. He is peeing all over my doorstep.

I never missed a beat. I handed him the business card and said, "Don't forget to put the * at the end of your gate code as I've written there. Have a good evening." I closed the door to the smell of the most rancid-smelling pee. This guy must eat asparagus every day. I can't believe this. He walked over to the gate controller, keyed in his code, and opened the gate. His friend was driving the vehicle and was pulling in now. He walked over to my closed door and screamed, "Thank you!" in the raspiest, hateful voice. Had this guy just peed on my doorstep to teach me a lesson? I'll show you for not letting me use your bathroom. I'll pee right here on your doorstep. For a split second, I felt guilty for not letting the unmasked man come in and use my bathroom. Maybe he had to pee THAT bad. But if that was the case, why didn't he go around to the side of the building where I couldn't see him or over to the fence? Right out front, where his car was parked, is a small wooded area. No. I think he peed on my doorstep to show me who's boss. To show me what I deserve for not letting him use my bathroom. He had been so hateful up to this point, and his screaming thanks at my door was the topper. I do think it was to teach me a lesson. I wonder what the guy he came with thought, having to ride home with Mr. Pee Pee Pants stinking to high heavens.

I waited until they had driven away to go out the door, and I hurriedly put my things in the car, locked up the office, and went out the gate. I didn't want to be confronted by him. He seemed a bit unstable.

Although he paid with a credit card, he insisted on coming to the office to pay his monthly bill. The payment could easily be made with a one-minute phone call, but he preferred to pay in person. He would remind me that his wife had passed away recently, and he was looking for a new woman. I told him that I already had a husband. I wanted to say, "Besides, I wouldn't date someone who pees on my doorstep out of spite." He said, "Well if you change your mind, you know where to find me." Yeah, I'll be all over that. Not!

Cheaper Than A Hotel

I had a customer who rented a 10 x 15 storage unit. I noticed that he would visit the storage unit three or four times a week. While not entirely unusual, it did catch my attention. He always arrived during the daytime, never after 5 pm, and would stay for an hour or two before departing. What struck me as odd was how he always parked his car right outside the door of his storage unit and would close the unit's door every time. Our storage units don't have electricity, so there was no lighting inside. Though I suppose he could have used a battery-powered lamp. Additionally, he was never alone, and each time he came, it was with a different woman. Curiosity got the better of me one day, so I planned a quick drive-by on my golf cart when he was there.

As expected, he arrived, and as he started keying in his gate code, I hopped on the cart. I timed my drive to coincide with the sound of his door opening. What I saw was unexpected. The storage unit was transformed into what looked like a motel room. There was a large bed adorned with bed linens, a plush comforter, and pillows. Flanking the bed were nightstands, each holding a lamp, though unlit due to the absence of electricity. It looked like a bedroom set from a TV show. It was clear this guy was using the unit for intimate encounters. I couldn't tell if the women were professionals or acquaintances.

. But, if they weren't professionals, he managed to persuade women to retreat to a storage unit for intimacy. This routine persisted for several months until one day. He gave notice. When I inspected the unit afterward, it was spotless and empty. I wondered if he had moved to another unit or perhaps decided to turn over a new leaf. He never used the unit for overnight stays, only for daytime rendezvous. It made me think that perhaps he had a significant other at home and this unit served as his secret escape. I can only speculate.

Drug Paraphernalia

Right after the South facility opened, I acquired a new customer who never put locks on his unit doors. He was renting a 10 x 30 storage unit with entrances on both ends. Opening both, you could get a refreshing breeze through the unit, even on the hottest summer days. A few months in, he fell behind on his payments. Since his units were always unlocked, I quickly checked the contents when he became delinquent. Inside, I found an array of brand-new items: 5-gallon buckets, clear hoses, timers, grow lights, boxes of baggies, and many gardening tools. Essentially, he had everything needed to start a large marijuana-growing facility. Our storage units don't have electricity, thankfully. I'd seen him removing items from the unit from time to time, suggesting this was likely just his stash of extra supplies. The actual setup, wherever it was, must have been large-scale, given the quality of the equipment in this unit.

I contacted a local sheriff deputy I knew, and we both inspected the contents. Unfortunately, without any direct evidence of drugs or residue – since all the items were brand new – there was nothing to act on. The deputy believed that the main growing operation must be somewhere else, as the stored items seemed to be backup equipment. I informed him that despite multiple requests to the customer to secure his items, he never locked the unit. Eventually, he settled his bill right before the contents were due for auction. After payment, he moved out, leaving some items behind. When I cleared out the unit, I unexpectedly found a crack pipe and several small bags of marijuana scattered on the floor. His confidence level was astounding; he'd stored not just paraphernalia but actual drugs in an unlocked unit.

I absentmindedly gathered the small bags and stored them on the dashboard of the golf cart, then discarded the remaining trash. A few months later, I had forgotten about the dashboard stash. The golf cart needed a battery replacement, so the owner, who was 81 years old, took it for service. After he left, I remembered the stash and called him, but he had already handed the cart over to the service center. To my surprise, when the cart returned days later, the marijuana was untouched on the dashboard. I pondered on whether the mechanics noticed and chose to ignore it or if they suspected the elderly owner was perhaps a bit more adventurous in his pastimes. The thought of him getting pulled over while transporting the cart and its illicit cargo was both amusing and horrifying. I could almost visualize the news headline:

"Eighty-one-year-old millionaire arrested for possession of over 4 ounces of marijuana."

The worst realization was that it would've been entirely my fault due to forgetting it was there in the first place.

Let's Play Dress-Up

I once had a customer who used his storage unit as a dressing room/photo booth for the longest time. He was a married man whose wife had no idea he was a cross-dresser. People in the community knew him and were sure his wife was clueless, although many of us knew about his "hobby."

I was told a story about him many years ago and completely ignored it. I assumed it was just a rumor and people were gossiping. He had an office next door to an HVAC service. One day, the guys at the HVAC office were returning from lunch and happened to glance through the front window of their neighboring business. They saw my customer wearing a wedding dress and admiring himself in a full-length mirror towards the back of the building in his office. At the time, I didn't understand why he would have left his office door open so that people out on the sidewalk could walk by and see him. The story seemed far-fetched. I disregarded it for years and had all but forgotten about it.

Fast forward many years later, he rents a storage unit from me. Actually, he rented two units. A large one that he kept his business items in. His business involved reselling and installing outdated cheap phone systems for local small businesses. He kept all the equipment for that business in one unit and then held a smaller one. One day I arrived at the storage facility a little earlier than usual. Like always, I drove around the facility to check on the fence, ensure there wasn't anything lying in the parking lot, and make sure the units were okay. I noticed one of the small doors open along the back side of the facility with no one around. Not seeing anyone in the unit or a car parked nearby, I assumed the worse. I thought someone had broken into the unit because the door was wide open. I got out of my car and stepped into the storage unit. Everything looked fine. It was so immaculate and organized that it gave off a weird vibe. I lifted a lid to a box to my right, and inside were bras and falsies—various sizes and colors in each shoe-box-sized container. The following few boxes contained wigs of different colors and lengths.

I peeked into one or two more boxes, and other than an unexplained creepy Hannibal Lecture/Buffalo Bill vibe, everything seemed fine and untouched. The last thing I noticed was a hanging bar with many dresses. They weren't your ordinary average dresses, though. One looked like the dress that Dorothy wore in The Wizard of Oz. Another looked like something Little Red Riding Hood would have worn. Each dress looked like something out of a child's storybook. While standing there looking up at the dresses, I was startled out of my stupor by someone asking, "Can I help you?"

After jumping out of my skin and composing myself, I asked, "Is this your unit?"

My little wedding dress-wearing friend answered, "Yes."

I told him I was driving by and saw the door open with no one around. He said he had walked over to his other storage unit for a moment and was coming back to close this one up.

I said, "Oh, that's good. For a moment there, I thought you had been broken into."

I got back into my car and went up to the office. As soon as I got back into my office, the wedding dress story came back to me, and I said to myself, "I'll be darned; he is a cross-dresser." I honestly didn't care, and he wasn't hurting anyone.

An hour or so went by, and he came into my office and told me everything in that storage unit belonged to his wife. He keeps it separate from his business items. He is telling me this because he thinks he's been busted. But I don't mind or care either way. He leaves my office, and that's the last I hear about it from him.

Weeks go by, and he is standing in my office telling me about some phone system that he was able to purchase from a place here locally that was upgrading their phone system. He wants to show it to me for some reason. I humor him mainly because I'm curious about his other storage unit and what he must keep there. It turns out it was mostly junk—lots and lots of outdated phone systems and stuff he had purchased through auctions. I did, however, notice a tripod and a photo backdrop. It's one where you can change the background by pulling down a new screen. It is similar to the systems used when your picture is taken in grade school. There was no camera on the tripod, but it was obvious that he had been taking photos there of something.

I began to have people stop by my office and tell me they noticed someone acting strangely. Walking up and down the aisle or just going into the next hall and walking around. Okay, this isn't a crime. It is concerning as there is no reason for someone to walk around the facility away from their unit. These few people tell me the person stops at the end of the row, looks at them, and returns where they came from. Again, nothing too alarming, just odd. Then, a couple came into my office after having moved out the weekend before. They wanted to talk to me about something they had seen the weekend they were moving out.

The couple's wife started by saying that she was concerned for my safety. She told me that while they were moving out, a man in women's high heels came around the end of the building, walked back and forth, and then walked away. Again, not a crime but odd. He just ensured he was seen and then returned to his unit. It came to me then that way back when he was trying on the wedding dress; he didn't close that door because he liked that someone might see him. Here he was, walking around in women's shoes inside the facility when people were there, in hopes of being seen. He wasn't coming out in full drag, but just enough to get a thrill from it and risk being seen. I told the couple that I knew who it was. I knew him personally, and it was okay. I wasn't in any physical danger; this was just his thing. The woman was pretty disturbed by it, though. This was before all the drag queen shows on television, and mainstream TV hadn't made cross-dressing a household name. Again, I assured her I was safe and appreciated her looking out for me.

I never said anything to him, but it bothered me a little that he was freaking out other customers. It wasn't very long at all before I got another complaint. This one was quite different from the other complaint. This time, the customer was quite vocal and upset. He came into my office to tell me that the next time that weirdo comes around the corner and looks at him, he is going to "Kick his ass." This guy was under the impression that our little guy was hitting on him or trying to. He told me this guy kept coming around the end of the building and looking at him wearing women's high-heeled shoes. He thought that maybe the other customer was hoping to hook up with him, and he wanted nothing to do with it. He told me the next time the guy "propositioned" him, he would "beat the shit out of him." Great. His prancing around in women's things would get him beaten up. I saw him a couple of days later and asked him to come into the office for a moment. I sat him down and tried to tell him in the nicest way possible to knock it off before something bad happened to him. I told him about the first couple being disturbed by his behavior. He immediately wanted to tell me his side of the story. He wanted to explain why it "wasn't what it looked like." I cut him off and said that I understood what he was doing wasn't hurting anyone but that keeping it in his storage unit would be best. I then told him I was bringing this up because someone had threatened to hurt him if he did it again and they saw him. He finally quit trying to make up excuses to explain his behavior away and left my office. Luckily, I never got another complaint after that.

He decided to move out of his storage units. He told me that business had dropped off, and he couldn't afford the storage units. He asked if he could leave a few things behind that were no longer needed, and I told him he could. I wanted him to move out to ease my concerns and make my life easier. He ended up leaving a bunch of stuff behind, and I was able to auction it off at the very next auction and didn't have to pay to have it hauled away. He had left some file cabinets behind, and the people who bought the storage unit came into the office after loading up to show me what they had found. They brought me twelve 8x10 glossy photos of him in each one of the outfits I had seen hanging up that day. They were all shot in front of those backdrops in his larger storage unit. In each picture, he wore thick white stockings, so his leg hair didn't show. However, he kept his mustache in each photo, which defeated the point. I still have those pictures and have no intentions of sharing them with anyone because they would serve no good purpose and only cause pain. They are good for comic relief, though.

"I Just Want My Pictures Back," Or Do You?

Quite a few years ago, I had a unit that went up for auction. I contacted the unit owners, and they received all the necessary letters. Ultimately, they said, "Go ahead and sell it because we can't come up with the money." Generally, if I have heard from the storage unit owners and they are attempting to make payments, the units will not get to the auction. It's better for us that the units not be sold, as it could open us up to lawsuits. Occasionally, though, we have done all we can, and we can't let them sit there unpaid forever. This was one of those units.

The day came with no fanfare, and the unit was sold to some regulars who attended every sale. They immediately began to empty the unit, which was a larger one packed full of household items. Two days after the auction, the couple's wife, to whom the unit had belonged, called. She asked if there was any way that I could sell her back her wedding dress. I explained to her that I didn't have it because the unit had sold at auction. However, I would communicate with the people who had bought her unit and see what I could do to help her. I never give out the names of the people who bought the unit because I don't want them to be harassed or bothered by the previous owners. I imagined it could get pretty messy, and indeed, it did.

After speaking to the buyers, they agreed to return her dress. It was a size 0 or 1 and a gorgeous dress with a small market. Plus, the people who purchased the unit were generous and kind and wanted to return it to her for its sentimental value. I called to let her know it was back, and after more than two weeks, she finally showed up to claim it. A few days go by, and she calls again, wanting a quilt or something like that from the unit. I told her I would inform the buyers but couldn't guarantee anything. She continued to call almost daily, sometimes twice daily, with a laundry list of items she was looking for out of the unit. It had gotten out of hand. Now, mind you, she never called me once when the unit was up for sale, not once calling to make any payment arrangements, but now she was blowing up my phone, offering $200 to $300 a pop for items. The buyers put together a box full of things for her, and she paid them $300.00 through me. Again, she took her time coming to get the items, which sat in my office, taking up space. When she came to get that box of articles, I told her they were compiling all the pictures and personal papers and would let her know when they were ready to be picked up.

Returning all the private documents and photographs from the unit to the owners is standard for our facility. In the meantime, she continued to call with requests for items that were getting pickier and pettier. I had no intention of asking the buyer for the additional items as they had already been quite patient and generous.

Finally, the day came when several boxes of photos and papers were brought back to the office. I called the wife and told her to pick them up as soon as possible, as there were quite a few boxes. The buyers told me there had been quite a few nude photos in with the bunch and made light of the situation. This is common. A few days later, she showed up, and I helped load the boxes into the back of her vehicle, and she was off. Whew, finally, I'm done with her.

Wait. Not so quick. The phone rings the next day, and I have a screaming, sobbing woman yelling at me. She is so angry and is screaming so much that I can hardly make out what she is saying. She says, "How dare you! Why would you do such a thing? As if losing all my stuff wasn't bad enough, and now this." I honestly had no idea what she was referring to. I asked what she was talking about. "The pictures, I am talking about the nude photos!" Okay, now I get it. She is embarrassed by the fact that the buyers have found her nudes. She could probably tell they had been looked at. Maybe they had been in an envelope, and now they weren't. I don't know. However, how would the buyers even know what they had were photos if they didn't look at them? I explained that the buyers didn't know her, nothing nefarious had been done with the pictures, and they returned them to her. I'm sorry they were in the storage unit for the buyers to find. None of that was her main concern. As it turns out, she's angry because the photos aren't of her. They are of her husband's ex-girlfriend. She is mad because the buyers had put them in with the rest of the pictures. Like they knew the difference, they had never met the woman. I had only met her once or twice, and believe me, her face wasn't the primary focus of the pictures. I stopped her right there.

"We have gone out of our way to get you back all the items that had sentimental value to you and returned all your photos. We had no idea that it wasn't you and the one you need to be mad at is your husband for having the photos in the first place. I'm going to hang up now, and I'm going to block your number. Our business is done here," I said.

That was the last time I spoke to her. I wonder how that worked out for her husband in the end. Yikes.

Chapter 7 Take The Good With The Bad

Just One Cardboard Box

Over the years, I have had many excellent, friendly, and kind customers. One, in particular, comes to mind. Every month, like clockwork, this customer would come in and pay his bill. He would hang around the office and visit for a while. He talked about being a rail enthusiast and having a brother. Mostly, he would discuss what he had done in the past month and his upcoming plans. They were super modest plans. He spoke about what he planned to watch on TV once the new seasons started or where he had gone to dinner. Nothing remarkable, but he liked to share his stories with me.

I honestly didn't notice his health going downhill. Many times, I can see when a regular customer's health begins to deteriorate. Often, they simply aren't getting around as well anymore. Their voice might be quieter, or breathing becomes more challenging. But I never noticed it with this customer. When he didn't show up for the next two months to pay his bill, I became concerned. I called his home but didn't get an answer, and I feared the worst. I was right. Another week passed, and I got a call from his brother. He let me know that his brother had passed away and while going through some of his things at the house, he noticed a rental contract with the facility. He was inquiring if the storage was still there and, if so, if he could come and check it out. He had no idea how much was in storage, but it had to be cleaned out eventually, and he wanted to get an idea of what that would entail. He paid the bill and arranged to come to the storage unit to check it out.

When he arrived, he stopped by the office to introduce himself before heading back to his brother's storage unit. Just a few minutes had passed before he returned to the office. He had a funny look on his face and began telling me he had a feeling that I might have been his brother's only "friend" here. His brother lived out of town, and although they spoke on the phone, it wasn't the same. He asked me how long his brother had been renting with me and how often he came to the storage unit. I told him he came every month on the third to make his payment and had been doing that for ten years. I never noticed that he ever went back to storage while he was here paying, and I checked the gate records to confirm that the only time he was there was on the third of each month. He hadn't come into the facility any other times, only when he paid his monthly rent. His brother asked me if I would come out to the storage unit for a moment so he could show me what his brother had been storing all this time. He spoke a little more about his brother. His brother would tell him he had gone to see Ginger that day. He would repeat a story or conversation we had had, and his brother just assumed that Ginger lived in his retirement complex.

We got to the unit; he had already removed the lock and raised the door. A small cardboard box sat inside this storage unit. It sat right in the dead center of the floor. He walked over and picked the box up, and inside were some old transit schedules. These were schedules of passenger trains he had traveled on. They weren't collector's items by any means; other than their sentimental value, they had none. His brother said, "I guess he just kept this box here so he could come in every month and visit with you—all these years for one little box of papers." I felt honored and guilty at the same time. I had taken his money month after month for all those years. I never knew that he had nothing in the storage unit and was renting it to come into the office each month to visit. We laughed, and he asked me if I could throw the box away for him. I said I would and felt a little pang of guilt as I dropped the worthless box of papers in the trash. He thanked me for being so kind to his brother over the years. And that was that.

Going Above and Beyond

I have developed friendships with a few customers over the years. Several are Facebook friends, and others I see and talk to outside of work. I often find myself going above and beyond for some of my customers. I'm somewhat of a captive audience and bad at saying "no."

I have a customer who lived in a home her brother owned for many years. It had been a rental property, but when she lost her husband and they hadn't planned for her independent living after his passing, she had to find affordable accommodations.

She hadn't worked outside the home during their entire marriage, so her social security was minimal. Since her husband had been self-employed, his social security was also lacking. Her brother offered her the use of his rental property, and she lived there for many years. It wasn't the worst place I had ever seen, but it wasn't ideal by any stretch of the imagination.

I met her the day she came to rent from me. She was distraught, and I could tell she was unsure about her next steps. Her brother had passed away, and shortly after the funeral, her nephew informed her that she needed to vacate the house by the end of the month. He planned to rent the house out, and she couldn't meet his asking price. She ended up moving into her sister's home. Although the sister's house was immaculate and in a better part of town, it was fully furnished. Her sister, being high-strung and suffering from OCD, found it difficult to cohabit. All of my customer's belongings had to be put in storage.

A few friends and I helped move everything from her home into storage, where it has remained for many years. She only retrieves a few sets of clothes at a time, rotating her wardrobe from the storage. She even keeps her weekly towels there, only bringing them home on laundry day, as her sister's OCD doesn't tolerate anything in the house except her own possessions. Although her sister has lived alone for a long time, set in her ways after her husband's passing, they somehow manage.

Over time, I've drafted legal letters and written references for her when she sought credit. She often discusses family matters with me, seeking advice or merely a listening ear. It's astonishing how my role has expanded beyond that of a storage facility manager for some customers.

A friend, who has since passed away, gifted me a desk sign that read, "The Doctor Is In 5 Cents," inspired by the old Charlie Brown cartoons. He thought it fit my office perfectly. Many have sat across from me, often in tears, sharing personal stories or problems. Sometimes they confide in things they probably shouldn't, but they seem to trust me. I often joke that there's an invisible sign on my forehead reading, "Tell me all about it."

Throughout the years, I've done a myriad of tasks for customers, including seamstress work, resume and cover letter writing, dictation, and even helping someone draft their dating site profile, complete with a photograph. And I suspect it won't be the last time.

Chapter 8 TMI

Starting to Date Again

I rented a storage unit to a man for a few years who suddenly passed away. As far as I knew, he hadn't been ill; his death was unexpected. I met his wife for the first time shortly after he died. She was visibly distraught and emotional. She informed me of his passing and mentioned that his family was eager to access his storage unit. I also learned that one of his brothers, a customer at the same facility, was keen on going through his late brother's belongings. He expressed his frustrations about the wife's reluctance, accusing her of selfishness. Such family disputes are unfortunately common in my line of work, and I've witnessed several. Some get uglier than others, but all are distressing. The brother eventually ceased his visits and complaints after a few months.

Fast forward about eighteen months, and the wife visited my office again. She shared that she was venturing into the world of online dating. I wished her well, hoping she'd find a genuine companion.

A few months later, she excitedly spoke about a man she'd connected with online. Their interactions, up to that point, were confined to texts and exchanged photos. She eagerly showed me several pictures of him: a strikingly handsome young man, appearing fit and refined. Instantly, red flags went up in my mind.

Without sounding disparaging, I should accurately describe the woman to give context. She was a middle-aged widow, understandably vulnerable after her recent loss. Physically, she was quite tall, exceeding 6 feet, and had a substantial build. She wore thick glasses, and her hair was a dry, grayish-white mop of curls. The very first time I met her, she reminded me of a character from "The Terminator."

The gentleman's frequent compliments, especially given their early stage of interaction, seemed out of place. Concerned about potential exploitation, I gently advised her to proceed cautiously. I reminded her that some people prey on the emotionally vulnerable, and her recent inheritance made her a likely target for opportunists.

She was convinced he wasn't like that and would make sure she went into this with her eyes wide open. I told her to watch after him asking her to send money so he could come to visit her. He, of course, lived a few states away. She told me what he did for a living and I reminded her that he could then afford his own ticket to see her and be sure NOT to give him any information he could use to access her personal information.

A month went by and she came to the office again to pay for the next month's rent on her storage. I jokingly asked her how it was going with Mr. GQ and she told me that, sure enough, he had begun to ask her for money to see her. I felt so bad for her that he was the scammer. I knew he would be all along, but I was glad she was wise enough not to send him a dime. She remembered what I had said and immediately broke it off when he started asking her to wire him money. I told her how sorry I was but glad she hadn't been taken any further advantage of. End of story? Not quite.

The very next month, she came and showed me a picture of a guy that she had also met online locally. He was the polar opposite of Mr. GQ. He wasn't a nice-looking guy at all and almost seemed a little on the nasty side. Perhaps it was a bad picture. Maybe he wasn't much to look at, but he would have a heart of gold. As long as he wasn't trying to scam her out of money, taking advantage of her situation and treating her well, who cares what he looks like? They had started texting and emailing each other and now they were talking on the phone. This was good. Mr. GQ had never once called her on the phone, raising a red flag. Apparently, this guy actually existed and was willing to talk on the phone with her regularly.

I wished her luck; she paid her monthly rent fee and went on her way. The next time I see her, she starts right out of the gate, telling me how her first and last date with the new guy went. First, for some reason, she doesn't even go out on a real date with him. She meets him at a hotel instead. She proceeded to tell me how he kept grabbing her nipples and twisting them until it hurt. She asked him not to do that several times, but he kept it up. At this point, I was worried that she would tell me she was raped or beaten by this guy, whom she had only just met and in a hotel room for sex, no less. She then told me that she wasn't going to go out with him again because she thought that the only thing he wanted from her was blow jobs with her teeth out.

Yep. She went there. She said he called her again a few days later and wanted to get together again, but she wasn't interested because she knew that toothless blowjobs were all he wanted. This is way more information than I ever wanted to hear about her date with this guy. I was expecting something like, "We went to Apple Bees and he was really nice and I will probably see him again."

Not I gave him BJ's with my teeth out and I think he liked that more than actually having sex with me. That was her complaint. She seemed to forget about him twisting her nipples until it hurt altogether. The fact that he did that at all and wouldn't knock it off was concerning enough. What can you expect, though, if your first date is sex in a cheap motel room? I tried to interject that she might have better luck if she took it slow and went on a few dates with someone, like to the movies or out to dinner first and get to know them that way first. She said she was disappointed and wasn't looking to go out with anyone any time soon again. I guess if those were my first two experiences right off the bat, I'd be pretty gun-shy too. I never heard about any of her dating adventures again after that. She might have actually given up, or maybe they got so much worse that she decided not to share the details with me.

I don't know if she's ever found love again. I hope that when she does, she keeps her teeth in until marriage.

Who did you say she left you for?

A friend once gifted me a desk plaque that read, "The Doctor Is In. 5 cents." This tale revolves around the individual who inspired that plaque.

One of my very first customers, who had been with us for around 12 years, was the central figure of this story. He was a handsome man, articulate and poised. Every so often, he would drop by the office for a chat.

One day, he walked in, visibly shattered. For over 11 years, he had shared a home with his girlfriend, moving in after selling his own place. Out of the blue, she demanded he leave. He inquired if I had a larger storage unit available, as he needed to relocate all his possessions from their shared residence. She was making him vacate because she'd found someone else.

The twist was that her new partner was moving in the very next week. As it turned out, she, a nurse at the Federal Penitentiary, had fallen for an inmate – a man imprisoned for murder, soon to be released on parole. This wasn't a spontaneous decision; the pair had been conducting what he referred to as an "affair" for over a year. One might wonder how intimate such a relationship could be behind bars, but it was compelling enough for her to overhaul her entire life.

The gravity of the situation was profound. Picture this: Your long-term partner not only ends the relationship but replaces you with a convicted murderer. Here was my customer, a refined, educated man with a steady job, sobbing in my office. The realization that he was being jettisoned in favor of a felon surely weighed heavily on his self-worth.

Diagnosing Kids With ADHD And Autism For Money

A few years ago, I started observing a concerning pattern. Young mothers were taking their children to physicians, seeking diagnoses for ADHD, Autism, and other disorders. The shocking part? They candidly confessed that their children didn't genuinely suffer from these conditions. The reason for this ruse? A monthly government stipend linked to the child's "disability."

Several mothers revealed they had to travel to Indianapolis to find a willing doctor. It seemed local physicians were unwilling to wrongly diagnose their child(ren) with ADHD or Autism.

However, one of the most heart-wrenching tales came from a young man around 19 years old. He approached me as a new customer, brimming with enthusiasm about joining the Air Force.

His dream was to soar the skies as a pilot. He shared that he had scored impressively in the Air Force's tests, qualifying him for any training he desired. With imminent plans to leave for boot camp and basic training, he wanted to store his belongings. I shared my own connection with the Air Force through my two daughters, who were Airmen. This young man's aspirations stood out; he was set to be the first in his family to join the military and post-service, he aimed to transition to commercial aviation. He seemed to have a clear vision for his future.

However, a couple of months later, he was back. His quick return puzzled me; I assumed he might be awaiting a training date. But the reality was different and disheartening. His dream of becoming a pilot was dashed because the military discovered a childhood ADHD diagnosis during their deeper background checks.

The backstory was even more tragic. To cope with financial strains, especially with an absent father, his mother had gotten him falsely diagnosed with ADHD when he was just a child. This diagnosis entitled her to an SSI check each month. Not stopping at that, she would procure and sell the prescribed ADHD medications, capitalizing on their popularity among college students who believed it enhanced their concentration. He, however, had never taken any of the medications since his mother knew he didn't truly need them. She had juggled multiple jobs and relied on the disability check due to the father's absence. It had never posed an issue until the military got involved. By the time he was recounting this story to me, tears welled up in his eyes. Although he bore no resentment towards his mother, recognizing her desperate measures to make ends meet, he couldn't help but feel devastated about the drastic turn his life had taken.

He told me he could work around this by going to a private doctor and running a battery of tests to prove he didn't have ADHD. His only insurance was through the military; the tests could not be done through military doctors. He would have to get his doctor to confirm that not only did he not have ADHD, but that he hadn't taken the medication for it either. This testing would take weeks, and he could not afford to pay out of pocket. Both facts could be used against his mother for welfare fraud. She collected a check for her son for all those years and never gave him the prescribed medications. He found himself between a rock and a hard place and had nowhere to turn. He was damned if he did and damned if he didn't. In the meantime, they would find him something else to do in the military, but it wouldn't be what he had hoped and dreamed of.

A neighbor lady once bragged to me about getting $2600 a month for her children, whom she had diagnosed with various illnesses, but complained that she had to take them to Indianapolis every three months. I had not yet heard of a case like the young man where this choice to have your kid misdiagnosed for a monthly check had come back to haunt the child. I'm sure we will hear more cases just like this in the coming years.

Chapter 9

Just Plain Pains in the Ass

Where are you located?

I had a customer on the phone just a few days ago. She started the conversation by asking me in a very scratchy voice, "Do you have any units open?" Okay, that's a perfectly normal question about a storage facility, but I needed more information if I was going to be able to help her. I asked her which location she was interested in.

She yelled at me, "Terre Haute!"

"Okay, but which location in Terre Haute are you..." I began to ask.

She cut me off by yelling, "Indiana."

"We have several locations in Terre Haute. Are you interested in the North, South, or the East location?"

"Where's the North location at?"

I give her the address of the facility.

"There ain't street like that in Terre Haute!

"My business has been on this street for over 16 years now, so I'm positive of the address."

I have to wonder why people choose to take this approach. Obviously, she didn't know there was a such a street in town. That's fine. There are only three things on this road: A restaurant, a car wash for which the street was named, and us.

She let me know that I was mistaken or lying to her. What purpose would it serve our business for me to lie about our location? She stated she wanted to rent at the North location and would be there shortly. Luckily, she has yet to figure out where we are located. I would definitely recognize her voice.

I Shouldn't Have To Sweat!

One day, I got a phone call from a customer who started the conversation by telling me I was lying and guilty of false advertising. He explained that he broke a sweat in his climate-controlled unit earlier in the day while going through some boxes and moving things around. He was pissed that he had broken a sweat while moving furniture in his unit. He claimed that we were liars and shouldn't be advertising that the units were climate-controlled when they weren't. I told him the temperatures were set to automatically never go below 65 degrees in the winter and never hotter than 75 degrees in the summer months. I chose these temperatures based on pharmaceutical needs and not on household furnishings. Pharmaceuticals have a much stricter set of temperatures, and you have to keep them warmer and cooler than you would ever have to keep household items and furniture. He continued to yell at me and said he still thought it was false advertising. I asked him what temperatures he had seen in our advertising. We have never put any temperatures in our advertising. Because we keep it much cooler in the summer and warmer in the winter than any ordinary household items would need, we saw no reason to advertise the temps. Of course, he hadn't seen any temperatures specifically noted, but had he been working at home in his front room, he wouldn't have had to sweat. I explained to him that the temperatures were not set for living conditions. Although I noted that household items did not need to have the temperatures set so tight, he was still angry with me and said that he would be moving out at the end of the month.

A year later, he was still there. He came into the office and asked me if I was married, and I told him I was. He said he didn't mean any disrespect by asking. Once again, a guy who doesn't seem to remember being a total d-bag to me. Even if I weren't married, that would be a hard NO.

Why Can't I Have It For Free?

Here's a real winner. My boss is currently in the hospital, and his son came in to help finish up some construction we have going on in his dad's absence. We were reviewing some items that must be completed when a lady with a U-Haul pulled up. She came into the office, and we began filling out her paperwork. After asking her what size she needed and getting her first month's rent set up, I asked her if she wanted to pay for August since there were only three days left in July rather than having to come back in to pay for August. She asked, "Why do I have to pay for August?" She had just told me that she would need the unit through the end of August, so it wasn't rocket science to figure out she would need it for the next month.

I explained that she was paying for the last three days of July and for the month of August. "I don't understand why I have to pay for August." Again, I told her that since she had a U-Haul full of stuff to unload right now, we would start her rental today, July 29th, which would only be $7.98 for the rest of July and then $80.00 for August. She replied, "I don't know why I have to pay for August." "You don't have to pay for August today if you prefer. You can come back in three days and pay for it then." "No! Why are you making me pay for August at all? It should be free."

We don't offer a free month's rent. We never offer specials like that because they aren't necessary for us to get business. I asked if she thought we were running a special or something. She said no. She just didn't want to have to pay for August.

It finally dawned on me what she was doing. She could see that I was busy with other customers coming in who were waiting in line, and the boss's son was waiting to finish up our business. In addition to that, my phone constantly rang while I was assisting her, and she heard me having to put people on hold due to the number of calls coming in. She was trying to play me. If she acted outraged and kept insisting that I not charge her for August, although she was going to be using the unit, over and over again, I would become frustrated and give in. Throw my hands up in the air and say, "Fine. Okay, you can have next month free." to get her out of the office and on with business. Little did she know that I had worked under pressure with the public in this job for over 18 years and for 13 ½ years, getting ripped a new one over the phone by disgruntled customers at Columbia House. I knew this game and wasn't going to give in. After another one or two more tries, she gave up and paid for August. The moment she left the office, the people in the office asked, "What in the heck was that?" "Why did she think she was entitled to August free?" "What a drama queen." Yep. But I can be just as stubborn, and although I was as lovely as anyone could have ever been to her, she still didn't wear me down and get her way. I win.

I Don't Know If I Want To Pay My Bill Or Not

I got a call from a lady asking how long before the gate would lock her out. We had just moved the gate because of some new construction. It wasn't working right and needed to be rewired. So, we set the gate to manual mode. You just push it open and pull it shut. She knew this.

She said, "I'm trying to decide if I want my stuff or if I'll just leave it there. Most of it's my son's stuff anyway."

Then she added, "I won't know until next week if I'm gonna

pay. I'll let you know."

She hadn't paid her rent, and half the month was gone. I've been doing this job for a long time, so I knew what she was up to.

I told her she could wait on the bill, but I was placing a lock on her unit anyway. She freaked out, screaming, "No, No, NO! Don't lock it. Hold on, I'll pay it now." And she did. She paid right then. I figured she was planning to take the good stuff and leave the junk. She knew the gate was open to everyone, and she thought she could use that. If she hadn't called and told me, I wouldn't have known. With the gate, like it was, she could've come in after I left, and I wouldn't have known she was moving without paying the months' rent. Dumb move on her part. It reminds me of when a child tells you not to look in their room because nothing's wrong. You know to immediately go check.

There's a Port-a-potty Right Out Front!
Each day when I get to work, I drive around the facility to check the perimeter. Occasionally, I find things like boxes or bags of trash. Most times, however, I come across empty drink bottles, bottles filled with tobacco spit, and bottles full of pee. Today, I stumbled upon a rather unpleasant surprise.

As I was driving, I noticed something lying in a pile near the fence. I stepped out of my car to inspect it. When I was about 10 feet away, a foul odor hit me. There, in the corner of the facility, lay a pair of men's soiled underwear and two long white socks.

There was no way I was going to put those items in my car and drive them to the trash bin. I continued driving and parked near the office, all the while contemplating how to get rid of the mess without causing an odor problem in our trash storage. Behind the office is a wooded area. And yes, that's exactly where I decided to dispose of the items. Using a picker-upper, I tossed the clothing into the woods. What other option did I have? We don't have regular trash pickup. The discarded items from customers are stored in a designated unit, and a few times a year, we haul everything to the dump in our truck. But placing those soiled clothes in there? I wasn't sure the stench would ever leave. I had never resorted to using the woods before. Usually, when customers toss things over the fence – and it happens quite often with items as big as tires – I go and retrieve them. But this time, I felt I had no other option. Maybe after several rain showers, the items might be cleaned enough to minimize the smell. Eventually, many months from now, I might consider putting them in the trash storage. It got me wondering if the person had a spare pair of pants. Given the state of those socks, I can't imagine their pants were any better. There's a port-a-potty right out front. Maybe next time, they'll think to use it.